I0625802

This book is a work of fiction. Names, characters, places, and incidents are products of the author's imagination or are used fictitiously. Any resemblance to actual events or locales or persons, living or dead, is entirely coincidental. This book contains graphic violence, death, dying, torture, explicit language, swearing, drugs, and is intended for mature audiences only.

Copyright © 2020 by Corey Cepeda
Published by:
Razor Sharp Publishing LLC
ISBN:978-1-7354160-0-7

Follow La Familia
www.thedelossantosfamily.com
Twitter: @Real_La Familia
Instagram: lafamilia_delossantos
Facebook: LaFamilia_De Los Santos

<u>Contents</u>

From the Author

I will never be able to find the exact words to say thank you to every single person that has bought or read my books and continue support me. There is no sufficient gratitude that can be shown or repaid. This has been and continues to be such a surreal journey for me bringing these characters to life and seeing how much everyone enjoys this story. This entire series is simply my dream that has manifested into reality.

I've had my fair share of struggles bringing them to life and lost focus at times. But every time I have begun to slow down, I remind myself no one is going to make this happen but me. I have to believe in myself first before anyone else will and that very simply is my message to all of you. Please don't EVER stop believing in yourself. Chase your dreams like you need air to breathe. Chase your dreams as if you are going to run out of air. There is only right now, there is only this moment, seize the opportunity it may never present itself again.

To everyone in the world with a dream no matter how big or small, protect it, feed it, and make it grow. Nurture it every day gently or slap it in the face. Whatever you decide, do not EVER give up on your dreams, be patient with it, but chase it with ferocity. The struggle is hard, and the war will be hell, however, the gratification of success will taste sweeter than anything you could have imagined.

<u>Dedication</u>

This book is dedicated to all of the magnificent people in my life that have directly or indirectly helped me along this incredible journey. My amazing family: Kirsten, Kaylee, and Payton, I love you! You have always given me strength to be a good man and do what's right in life and honor you. To my remarkable mother who raised a son alone and worked two jobs to put food on the table and clothes on my back. My father who worked his way back into my life at the age of fourteen, when I would need him the most. He mended our broken relationship and helped to guide me in life. To John Turnipseed, Thornton "TJ" Jones, and VJ Smith, outstanding men that God introduced to me at the perfect time when I was at my lowest. They helped save me . . . I am eternally grateful! Lastly, I need to mention William Jones. I witnessed him commit so many unspeakable acts of violence against my mother for so many of my young, impressionable years. He beat, slapped, punched, and almost choked her to death right in front of me. He called her disgusting names and belittled her, stripping her of her dignity, from which she still suffers. It had taken me many decades of deep soul searching to understand why I had to witness this as a child. One day, well into my mid-thirties, it hit me like an epiphany: I was not placed into those situations to be hurt or harmed, but to see what a man is and is not, how to treat people with respect, and cherish those you love. Despite all of his evils, I grew to have an incredible life and become a man with deep passion, love, and forgiveness. I am the opposite of what he was. Upon learning of his passing many years ago, I did not feel the need for closure I had already forgiven him.

Acknowledgements

It is a great honor to acknowledge and say thank you to all of our military men and women for your outstanding service to our country. You have made and continue to make such unbelievable sacrifices for this country and our freedoms. To our brave police officers across the entire United States of America that keep our cities and counties safe, I say thank you as well. I need to pay tribute to all of the mentors and trail blazers in the world that I have not shared space with but who have continually inspired me to just be great. In their own ways, they have helped me to realize that I needed to "jump" and allow my parachute to open, to get out of my comfort zone and be brave, to be the hardest worker in the room, move forward when my back is against the wall, do not let my past dictate my future. It is o.k. to fail, failure means growth, and no matter how many times I get knocked down, I just simply need to get back up. I have learned to lead by example because you never know who is watching. Be the light in someone else's life you will shine brighter. I have learned I only have this life and I will live it to the fullest! I have been deeply inspired to allow my writer's voice to flow freely, believe in myself and write unapologetically, to trust my content and speak with depth and confidence. So, to Steve Harvey, Tyler Perry, Bishop TD Jakes, Gary Vaynerchuk, Dwayne "The Rock" Johnson, Terry Crews, Kurt Sutter, Vince Gilligan, Daymond John, Creflo Dollar, Vince Flynn, Muhammad Ali, Will Smith, Magic Johnson, Michael Jordan, Kobe Bryant, Dr. Dre, and Quincy Jones, Oprah Winfrey, Tony Robbins, Joyce Meyer, JK Rowling, Nelson Mandela, Dr. Martin Luther King Jr., I say thank you for your lifelong inspiration!

<u>Prologue</u>

The De Los Santos family has just been savagely attacked! In an unprecedented act of cowardice, the brazen assassination attempt at Lucita's 10th birthday party went horribly wrong, slaughtering dozens of women and children. Catapulting into motion a series of events that can never be undone. A merciless drug dynasty in Mexico for over fifty years, they are now in critical danger of being ripped to shreds as they struggle between their loyalties to the drug empire they have built and with one another.

Vicente, The Boss of Bosses severely injured, will have his throne challenged not just by his enemies but by his own flesh and blood as he recovers. Ignacio, Vicente's oldest and power-hungry son, races to locate those responsible for the bombing while waiting impatiently in the shadows for his opportunity to be king. Hot on his heels Aurelio, a powerful Lieutenant in the Sinaloa State police, and Vicente's brother. He will investigate the tragic events of the day, quickly realizing that something very sinister lies deep beneath the surface.

Gabriella will look to extract unimaginable revenge, while balancing the needs of her beautiful daughter and injured husband. Santino rushes home to provide support to his family only to be sucked in the middle of their dysfunctional relationships. Bonds will be severed, alliances challenged, and hearts will be destroyed. Bloodshed and collateral damage will ensue when war is declared on and within the De Los Santos family.

Chapter 1: The Birthday Party

Women were screaming, holding their bloody children. Thick gray smoke filled the air—It was heavy and blinding. It devoured the land, moving in slow, as continuous waves crashing across the landscape. It gradually filtered its way up, crossing the beautiful sun-filled sky. Rubble lay on the ground, people screamed and moaned in agony, the muffled chaos inside his head sounded like incoherent chatter.

Small fires burned all around him. Tables and chairs toppled over, presents still ablaze. He tried to lift himself up off the ground but could not, feeling disoriented from the ringing in his ears. His face covered in dirt and debris, not able to catch his breath, coughing and choking from the smoke. It all seemed like a slow-motion movie.

Trapped under a small table; it appeared to weigh a ton. He slowly rolled over to his back, pushing the table off to the side. He struggled to get to his feet, stumbling, finally gaining his composure. He looked around, trying to make sense of what had happened, hearing voices all around him unable to decipher the unintelligible sounds being spoken.

Men ran around with guns, trying to pick up the wounded. He surveyed the area while holding a gash on the side of his head, still bleeding profusely. As he looked across the pool area, he saw the unimaginable. He thought the unthinkable—*I have been attacked!*

Vicente De Los Santos strolled across the deck of the patio, stepping over the mangled bodies that lay at his feet. It was pure chaos and destruction. Suddenly, a tall slender man ran up from behind him, grabbing him by his waist,

"Jefe! Jefe!" he screamed, "We must depart, we must leave now!"

La Familia: Loose Ends

It was Diego, Vicente's second in command. The terror in Diego's voice, along with the utter sense of urgency in his tone, expressed to Vicente how dreadful the situation seemed. However, Vicente De Los Santos was a man that would not run; retreat did not exist in his genetic makeup.

A proud man with a warrior's heart and a fighting soul at this very moment, he needed to take control of the matter.

Vicente pushed Diego away.

"Go and find my son. Find out where he is!"

"But Boss, we must leave now! I must keep you safe!"

"Go and find my son, you idiot! Ignacio will keep me safe!" Vicente screamed back at him.

"When you find him, meet me back here!"

As Vicente barked out the order, he fell to one knee, his head still ringing from the bomb blast. His ribs hurt like hell and more than likely were broken. He struggled to not completely collapse to the ground, using a table to help steady himself.

"Very well, Boss, then please take this. I'll find him."

Diego handed Vicente his machine gun, then pulled out a black 9mm Beretta from the back of his waistband, cocking back the hammer. Diego then made his way back through the smoke and carnage.

Vicente forced himself to his feet. Wrapping the leather strap of the AK-47 around his shoulder, he shook his head to clear the cobwebs preparing for battle. His first thoughts became of his family. His wife, Gabriella, was she alive? And his precious daughter, Lucita. He shuddered at the thought of anything happening to her.

Vicente slowly started shuffling back through the pool area, which now resembled a war zone. He had a slight limp in his right leg. All around him, bodies lay motionless, floating in the swimming pool, which had now turned bright crimson red from the blood of the dead.

Vicente gripped his weapon firmly in both hands, ready for anything, although most of the surrounding people had died or were too wounded to pose a threat.

"Gabriella!"

Vicente screamed out with terror and dismay in his voice.

"Gabriella!"

He screamed out again but this time louder, spinning in a three-hundred-sixty-degree motion to see all around him. Vicente heard no response, just the crying and moans from the survivors laying on the ground, begging for help.

Vicente had to shut out the noise of the wounded. He had to drown out the cries of those dying. All he cared about was finding his queen, his Gabriella. Vicente limped back to where he was when the bomb went off, where both he and his wife had been standing.

The smoke cleared for a moment when Vicente saw a figure laying on the ground. He limped over to the female body, kneeling down beside her, hoping to see his wife and that she would still be alive. He reached down and grabbed the woman by the shoulder, rolling her over. It wasn't Gabriella.

Just then, Vicente detected a faint cry in the distance. His head shot up, his eyes grew big, his heart filled with terror. He recognized that cry instantly, but it was not his wife's—no, the moment had become much, much worse. The cry sent sheer panic through his bones; realizing the sounds of his beautiful 10-year-old daughters' voice, Lucita.

Vicente hobbled toward the tiny voice yelling,

"Lucita! Lucita! Mi Niña!"

When Vicente reached her, she was sitting amid a pile of rubble.

Relieved to see that she was okay, however, she appeared to be in an extreme state of shock. Dead bodies lay all around her.

La Familia: Loose Ends

Vicente could smell the vulgar odor of burning flesh, which meant more than likely she smelled it too. She sat on the ground, crying uncontrollably.

Her beautiful white dress now dirty and torn, her hair mangled and strewn all over her face. Lucita's once perfect makeup now ran down her face with her tears.

"Why did they do this, Papá? Why?" she cried as she reached out to him.

Her pretty white gloves now soiled black from the dirt and soot. Vicente grabbed his daughter, pulled her close to him, and wrapped his arms around his vulnerable princess.

"I don't know, my love. I don't know mi Amor." Vicente said to his wounded daughter's heart. But in the back of his mind, he knew precisely why they had been attacked. He was being challenged, he was being tested, someone wanted to take what he had worked so hard to build, his empire!

"Come, Lucita, we must go. I must get you to a safe area."

Vicente attempted to pick her up but grimaced as the pain in his leg had gotten worse, and his ribs still hurt.

"Are you okay, Papá?" Her fragile little voice asked.

"I am fine, Lucita, but we must go."

Vicente held his daughter around her waist with his left arm and steadied his machine gun with the other. He pointed it straight through the smoke, ready to kill anyone in his path.

As they made their way toward the house, Vicente saw to his left the door to his library and pointed with the weapon that they should walk in that direction.

Lucita and Vicente made their way into the house. The library consisted of a spectacular display filled with thousands of vintage books, high-end furniture, and hunting trophies.

Corey Cepeda

The room was besieged with lions, zebras, hyenas, and magnificent grizzly bears; all trophies collected over the years by the super predator himself, Vicente De Los Santos. He helped Lucita to the brown leather couch and kneeled in front of her. He brushed the hair out of her face and placed both of his hands on her cheeks.

"You need to listen to me, Lucita. I need you to stay here. I have to find your mother."

Lucita stared back at her father with no response; her eyes glazed over with emptiness.

"Lucita, did you hear me? I need you to stay here. I have to go and find your mother."

Vicente leaned in, giving his daughter a gentle kiss on her cheek.

"I know you don't understand what's going on, but you need to trust me right now. The safest place for you is here in this room. Stay here, Lucita. I'll be back soon."

Lucita sat on the edge of the couch motionless, staring off into the distance. Vicente realized she may not have been hurt physically, however, she appeared to be destroyed emotionally, but for the moment, she would be safe here. He stood back up and gave his daughter one last kiss on the forehead and walked back to the door.

Cracking the door open ever so slightly, Vicente slowly poked his head out, looking to his right and then to his left. The smoke had cleared from the pool area. He could see the bodies of his guests laying all around. Vicente exited the library, closing the door tightly behind him and limped slowly back to where the explosion occurred.

This time he held the AK-47 tight. Now starting to feel the deep murderous rage swell within him at the dogs who dared attack him at his own home.

Who would have the balls to do this to me and on this day? Who would know when and where to attack me? Who would benefit from this? The answer to that last question seemed simple—who would benefit from him being dead? Everyone.

La Familia: Loose Ends

Vicente crept slowly among the dead—little boys dressed in their tuxedos, and little girls in their pink outfits lay motionless. Friends Vicente had grown up with had now passed on to the next life awaiting judgment for their sins. He looked among the bodies, still trying to find his wife. In the distance, police sirens filled the air.

Vicente realized that it would only be a matter of minutes before the state and local police would be on his property.

He had to find Gabriella.

"Gabriella! Gabriella! Where are you, mi Amor?"

He was becoming frantic.

"Papá!" a man screamed, with a deep and familiar voice.

Vicente swung his body around, relieved to see his son, Ignacio, racing toward him. Ignacio was Vicente's oldest son and his grim reaper. Throughout his entire life, Vicente had groomed and prepared his own son to be a cold-blooded killer, an assassin.

When Vicente needed to settle any disagreements with rival cartels, he always turned to Ignacio. Ignacio grew to become his father's top lieutenant and kept all the other soldiers in line. Everyone within the De Los Santos cartel explicitly understood if they did not follow orders they would answer to Ignacio.

Ignacio came running up to his father just stopping short, a concerned expression crossed his face.

"Papá, you're hurt." Ignacio said as he looked at the wound on Vicente's head.

"I need to get you help. The police will be here any minute. I need to get you out of here!"

"No!"

Vicente yelled at his son.

"I have to find your mother!"

Ignacio paused.

"I will find her, Papá. I swear to you on my life, but I must get you out of here now!"

Vicente could feel his body beginning to shut down. His head now pounding out of control. He had lost a lot of blood from the wound on his head, plus putting weight on his bad leg had become a struggle. Vicente stood there staring at his son, so many thoughts racing through his mind.

Finally, Vicente reached out and grabbed Ignacio by the collar of his shirt.

"Very well," Vicente responded, angry at himself for showing weakness.

"You find your mother; you hurry and find her. Do you understand me? You find her and bring her to me!"

Vicente pushed and pulled on Ignacio's shirt forcefully, leaving no doubt how serious he was. Ignacio nodded and called out for his men to take his father with them.

"There is one more thing," Vicente said.

"Your baby sister is in the library. She is safe, but she is horribly shaken. When you find your mother, get them both out of here."

Ignacio nodded and then turned to his men that had now gathered behind him.

"You two!" he commanded, pointing at two of the closest men standing next to him.

"Take my father to the compound. Call the doctor and tell him to be ready."

They hurried forward, each man allowing Vicente to lean on them, then escorted him away. Ignacio pointed to another man carrying an Uzi submachine gun.

"You! Get to the library and stay with my sister. If anyone but me knocks on that door, you kill them!"

When the two men carrying Vicente reached the shiny black Mercedes Benz S350 parked in the driveway, Vicente stopped and looked back at his son one last time. As they locked eyes with each other, Ignacio interpreted precisely what his father was saying to him. *There will be hell to pay!*

Ignacio watched and waited as the Mercedes drove off down the dirt road, kicking up a cloud of dust. As it disappeared from view, Ignacio set off to find his mother, the matriarch of the family.

"Ignacio! Ignacio!"

Ignacio stopped and turned around to see Diego rushing toward him. In addition to being second in command in the De Los Santos army, Diego was Ignacio's best friend growing up. Diego had been the only man that Ignacio trusted. But friends or not, Diego understood if he was given orders, he had no choice but to follow them.

Diego earned the reputation of being just as ruthless a murderer and cold-hearted as Ignacio.

"Come," Ignacio said, "help me find my mother."

They headed off in the direction of the pool. As they made their way around the corner of the house, Ignacio stopped holding up his hand, signaling for Diego to stop.

He stared across the front of the pool area as Diego stood behind him, Diego turned to stand back to back with Ignacio. They had a complete view of the area, Ignacio pulled from his holsters, two shiny silver custom-made .45 caliber guns.

Diego held a menacing black Sig Sauer MG338 machine gun with a variable scope lens. Ignacio reached behind, tapping Diego on the leg, pointing in the table's direction where the explosion had occurred.

"Come, let's go over that way," Ignacio whispered.

The two men walked in tight formation with only a few feet between them, sweeping in a tactical motion with their weapons. By now, most of the cries and screams had stopped. Those who had survived the blast had gathered up their families and made their way to their vehicles, leaving the De Los Santos home.

It was hauntingly quiet, such a stark contrast to the music, singing, dancing, and joy that had taken place just a short while ago. No more laughing children, no more music, only the absolute silence of death. The two men reached the location where Vicente and Gabriella had been sitting before the explosion. Ignacio stopped and swung around to face Diego.

"I want you to cover the grounds down by the fence. I'll head around to the front of the house. Meet me back here in ten minutes."

Diego nodded and walked away. As he made his way through the mangled mess of the enormous patio area, he felt a hand grabbing his ankle. It scarred the shit out of him, causing him to jump back and point his weapon at the ground.

"What the fuck!" he screamed.

Diego looked down to see a small, bloody, dirty hand wrapped around his ankle, a hand of a woman. Diego crouched down, pushing some debris away. It was Gabriella covered in dirt, trapped underneath rocks and chairs, her white outfit unrecognizable, stained with her own blood and the dirt from the explosion.

"Ignacio! Ignacio!" Diego called out in a panic.

"I have her!"

Diego frantically began clearing away the debris. Once beautifully wrapped, children's presents were now destroyed. He shoved the broken chairs and a table to the side.

"It's okay, Señora De Los Santos. It's me, Diego. You are safe now, I've got you."

Gabriella positioned on her back, tried to open her eyes, but her face was covered in dirt. Diego swung his weapon across his shoulder and stepped over her. He put an arm behind her back to help her sit up, bleeding slightly, she was still alive. She appeared shaken and unsteady.

"Are you hurt, Señora? Are you badly injured?"

She looked at him blankly then shook her head to stop the ringing in her ears, but that only made it worse.

By now, Ignacio had made his way to his mother. The look in his eyes screamed panic and relief.

"Mamá, are you okay? Please, let me help you."

He handed his guns to Diego and then bent down, wrapping his arms around his mother to help her to her feet just as she collapsed into him. Diego stepped to the side. Ignacio turned to his mother and looked into her eyes.

She stared back at him in a daze, trying to focus. Then she cracked a slight smile.

"Ignacio," she said in a small, calm voice.

"Yes, Mamá, it's me. Are you okay?"

Gabriella placed her hand on his shoulder and steadied herself. She forced herself to clear her head.

"I am fine, Hijo," she responded.

Feeling a sudden panic, she cried out, "Where is Lucita? Where is your father? What happened?"

"They are all safe, Mamá. I sent Papá to the compound, and I have someone guarding Lucita. She's in the library waiting for you."

"And our guests?" she asked.

Ignacio paused. He did not have it in him to break his mother's heart with that answer—almost all of her friends were dead. He did not want to lie to his mother, but understanding it was the correct thing to do.

"They have been taken out of here. They are safe too."

She smiled back at him and placed her hand on his cheek.

"My Ignacio, my protector!"

"Come, Mamá, we must go. The police are on their way." Ignacio swung around to his mother's side, keeping his arm wrapped around her. She gathered her senses but was still very unsteady.

"Diego, get my car and bring it around."

Diego shot off to the front of the house.

"We must get Lucita," Ignacio said to his mother. He slowly guided her through the maze of carcasses strewn all over.

"I've got you, Mamá," Ignacio reassured his mother. As they made their way to the door of the library, he called out.

"Estamos en La Puerta!"

The door opened slowly, and a large menacing man with a long scar down his face stuck his head out of the door. He stepped back to make room for Ignacio and Señora De Los Santos. Diego followed behind. As they entered the room, Lucita looked up and ran over to them.

"Mamá!" she screamed.

"I am fine, little one."

Gabriella replied.

Lucita waited as Ignacio helped Gabriella to a chair. Then she sat down on the floor next to her, placing her head in her mother's lap.

"Look at me, Lucita."

She lifted her head up and stared into her mother's beautiful brown eyes. However, Gabriella struggled immensely as she stared back, studying her daughters face. She knew her special day had been destroyed. All the dirt and smudged makeup made her little brown face unrecognizable now.

"Lucita, are you hurt?"

"No Mamá, I am fine, but my friends. . . are my friends all dead?"

"No, my dear, they have been hurt. They are being looked after."

"No Mamá, I saw them, they were covered in blood. They were laying on the ground dead, they weren't moving!"

"Lucita, you must listen to me. Your friends are okay. Some of them might be hurt, but they are okay."

"I'm sorry, Señora. De Los Santos," Diego interrupted, still standing near the door.

"But we must go now. The police are coming. They'll be here in a few minutes."

"Diego's right," Ignacio said.

"We must get you out of here."

By now, the ringing in Gabriella's head had stopped, and she was thinking clearly.

"Ignacio, I will stay behind and deal with the police," she said resolutely.

"No, Mamá, you can't!" Ignacio snapped back.

"Papá was very clear. I needed to find you and bring you and Lucita to him. We must go!"

Ignacio demanded.

Gabriella placed her hands on his shoulders.

"Someone needs to stay behind and handle this. Are you going to do it? Are you going to talk to the police?"

She looked over at Diego and barked at him with a stern tone,

"What about you, are you going to fix this?"

Diego looked down at the floor, knowing he shouldn't answer.

Gabriella lowered her tone.

"I have to be the one to put this shit back together. Me! You've done your job. You found me. Now, take your sister to your father. Tell him I am okay, but I stayed behind to deal with this fucking mess!"

"Papá will not like this, not at all!"

Ignacio said with an expression of fear in his voice.

"If I leave you behind with the police, he will skin me alive!"

"Don't be ridiculous. He'll understand why I stayed behind. Now, all of you get out of here and go to your father!"

Ignacio stood staring at his mother, knowing he was in an impossible position. His father was the head of their empire, and his mother was not to be trifled with either.

"Ignacio!"

Gabriella hollered at him, snapping him back into reality.

"Take your sister and get the hell out of here!"

"Yes, Mamá," he relented.

"Diego, you will stay with me," Gabriella snapped.

Ignacio took Lucita's hand and headed for the door. He turned back and looked at Diego.

"Use the satellite phone to stay in touch. Call me the second this place is clear, then get out of here. And watch her!"

Diego nodded his head, knowing the principal responsibility he had just been given.

Ignacio and Lucita followed the guard who had been posted at the door. They quickly made their way to the driveway where a super-reinforced shiny pearl white Maybach Zeppelin awaited them. They all climbed in the vehicle and quickly sped away as Diego watched them drive off.

Gabriella walked over to a desk in the room and sat down. She pulled out a mirror and grabbed a tissue and began wiping the dirt from her face. She ran her hands through her hair and did her best to brush the dirt from her outfit. However, nothing she tried would remove the bloodstains. She sat, staring at herself in the mirror. What was she going to tell the police?

"Señora De Los Santos," Diego said.

"Are you okay? Can I get you something?"

"For the time being, I am fine, Diego. I need to figure out what I will say when the police arrive."

La Familia: Loose Ends

She despised the fact that the police would come onto her property and ask questions, but she knew there was no way around it.

Gathering herself, Gabriella put the mirror away and stood up, smoothing her clothing. She walked out of the library and made her way out to the patio. She stopped dead in her tracks, looking around at the carnage and devastation the day had brought. Diego stood behind her, awaiting his next order.

Inevitably, several local and state police vehicles arrived on the scene. They raced up the driveway, pulling off onto different parts of the De Los Santos lawn. Dozens of men wearing heavy body armor and tactical gear poured out of the vehicles, carrying M-16 rifles. They scattered in different locations to secure a perimeter around the property.

As the police cars filtered in, one car, a black Dodge Charger drove directly up to the front of the pack. It stopped at the very top of the driveway. Fashioned with dark tinted windows, it looked very different from the rest of the vehicles.

The passenger side door swung open, allowing a man to step out. With his black hair slicked back, the back of his bullet-proof vest read "POLICIA." He appeared to be in his early to mid-50s.

Listening to the frantic radio chatter in his earpiece, he adjusted the plastic to make it fit better. He wore dark aviator sunglasses, a black muscle shirt, formfitting, tight around his arms, along with two Walther P99 AS 9mm handguns, one strapped around each leg.

Leaving his car door open behind him, he walked around the front of his vehicle and turned to a smaller man who exited the driver's side door.

"Make sure they set the perimeter. No one in or out, not without my say so!"

"Yes, sir," the other man replied.

The officer removed his glasses, folded the bows, and tucked them into the collar of his shirt. He squinted his eyes a bit, the sun shined right at him. He gazed at the smoldering piles of debris that had been birthday presents. He stared at the bodies laying on the ground and took a moment to mentally process the catastrophe.

Gabriella had watched as he arrived. She crossed her arms in front of her as the officer turned and headed toward her. As he walked closer, his expression remained blank. He stopped just in front of her, looking her up and down. He took a quick survey of her physical state.

"You sure look like hell." he said with a deep booming voice.

"I feel like hell." Gabriella replied.

She took a step back. The officer now too close for her own personal comfort. She stared back at him with her head tilted slightly, not giving away any of the thoughts she had running through her mind.

"Is my niece okay?" he asked. "Are you okay?"

Gabriella uncrossed her arms and placed her hands firmly on her hips.

"Hello, Aurelio."

Her tone was pleasant; she had no reason to be rude. She accepted she was in no position to try to stir the pot.

"Lucita is fine. She's shaken up, but she is safe. I am fine."

Aurelio's cracked a slight smile, revealing his perfectly white teeth.

"Good." he replied.

He walked past Gabriella and moved to the pool area. Even as a seasoned professional, he had seen the worst humanity had to offer. Decapitations, mass graves however, the sight of dead children made him angry, something he could never get used to. Aurelio stood at the top of a small staircase as he looked out over the area. What savagery, what brutal destruction. A bomb blast at a child's birthday party, unspeakably heartless.

Aurelio stepped down making his way through the crime scene. His right hand placed on his holster, ready to draw his weapon if needed. Mostly a knee-jerk reaction based on all his years of training. He stopped in the middle of the pool area and swung back around to stare at Gabriella. He raised both of his arms out to his sides.

He asked, "Do you even want to try to explain this?" With a sound of disgust in his voice.

Gabriela crossed her arms again.

"Isn't it obvious? Someone tried to assassinate us. Someone tried to kill my family . . . Our family!"

"The bomb blast could be heard miles away," Aurelio replied.

"I was sitting at my desk watching a soccer game when I heard the explosion. You're lucky to be alive. This is much more than just an assassination attempt, Gabriella. This is an attempt to annihilate your entire bloodline and anyone connected to you. Anyone that does business with you. Hell, even anyone who has ever looked at you!"

Aurelio paused to once again to take in his surroundings. This time throwing up his arms.

"Just look at this . . . Look! Dead children, Gabriella, babies! There are people you've known your entire life, and now they're gone!"

He bent down and picked up one of the burned dolls.

"You see this?" This doll was probably held by a little girl whose life just got wiped out simply because she knew you or was friends' with Lucita! This isn't just about your family, Gabriella. This is about these innocent little lives that were stolen today!"

Aurelio barked at her.

"Whoever did this has the mind of a psychopath with absolutely no sympathy, no compassion, no emotion, no remorse, and I need some fucking answers!"

Gabriella leered at Aurelio with contempt. *Who is this pendejo to talk to me like this? How dare he?* She thought. However, in her heart, she knew he was right. Beautiful, innocent little lives had been lost, and she was in no position to fire back at him.

"I do not know, Aurelio, who would do this. Truly, I don't."

Her tone somber.

"My heart is broken for these beautiful little souls."

Gabriella repositioned herself, standing at the top of the small staircase.

Aurelio still holding the burned doll in his hand, placed his foot on the bottom step. He stared into her eyes,

"I believe you, but I still need answers. Your guest list would be an excellent place to start."

Aurelio handed the burned doll to Gabriella and walked past her back toward his vehicle. Gabriella stood there, holding the doll as she surveyed her surroundings. She wanted to cry. As a mother, this devastated her. But her loyalty remained to her family, feeling grateful that they were all alive.

She turned around and looked at Diego, who was still standing in the library's doorway.

"Call Ignacio, give him an update. Let him know we will be leaving shortly," she said.

Diego nodded disappearing back into the library, closing the door behind him. Gabriella walked over to Aurelio.

"I will get you a list of all our guests today, but it will take me a while," she paused.

"I do not have it here."

Aurelio was finishing a conversation on the phone.

"Yes, Commander, Entiendo."

He hung up, looked at Gabriella and chuckled.

"You must think I am an idiot, but I don't have the energy to argue with you. I have a crime scene to process. I will expect something by the end of the day. You are free to go."

Diego walked out of the library stopping right behind Gabriella.

"I have updated Ignacio, Señora."

"How is Vicente?" she asked.

"The doctor is attending to him right now."

"Very well, thank you." she replied.

Diego escorted Gabriella past the police vehicles to the garage area at the front of the house. Diego opened the passenger door of a stunning ruby red Rolls Royce Sweep Tail. Gabriella stepped inside; Diego closed the door behind her.

He walked around to the driver's side climbing in, starting the engine with a single touch of a button. The motor softly growled. As they approached the front gate, the entrance was blocked by two police vehicles. The men standing guard radioed up to Aurelio for permission to let them pass.

"Yes, let them go," he responded.

Gabriella felt a small bit of relief at finally being able to put some distance between herself and this horrific day. Now she too could see to her husband.

CHAPTER 2: The Aftermath

The metal doors of the infirmary flew open, two men carrying big black machine guns rushed in, holding a limping Vicente. The room was dimly lit, with only a few lights hanging from the ceiling to illuminate the space. Constructed of clay and old red brick, it made the air heavy and damp.

The doctor, who had been sitting at his desk waiting patiently, stood up and walked over to the old metal gurney.

"Get him on the table!"

The doctor shouted as the two men helped Vicente onto the table.

The doctor recognized immediately that if Vicente De Los Santos needed help, something terrible had happened. Vicente grunted as he hoisted himself up, he was in excruciating pain. His knee was terribly swollen. The bleeding from his head had stopped, but he looked pale.

"Here, lie down on the table," the doctor said, speaking softly.

"Lay back, my friend, let me see what those animals have done to you."

He first examined the wound on Vicente's head. The injury a crescent moon-shaped gash, was deep, leaving a flap of skin that barely stuck to his skull. The doctor tilted Vicente's head to the side to get a better look at it.

He touched the wound with a gloved finger to assess the damage but unintentionally reopened the gash, sending a thick stream of blood spraying out, hitting the doctor in the face.

The doctor maintained his calm, wiping his face on his sleeve. This is what he got paid very well to do—work on emergency cases, in less than ideal conditions, for the De Los Santos family.

"You!" he shouted to one of the men.

"Bring me that gauze and the bottle of peroxide; it's right next to you."

The sizeable man grabbed both items and made three quick steps to the doctor.

"Open it up, give it to me. Hurry!" The doctor ordered.

The man tore open the package and handed it to the doctor.

"This is going to hurt a bit, Vicente."

He reached over and grabbed the small brown bottle of peroxide, saturating the gauze with it, placing it on Vicente's wound.

"Fuck!" Vicente screamed.

"Give me something for the pain!"

"Here, hold this," the doctor directed the man who was standing next to him.

"Apply steady pressure."

The doctor turned to open an old white medicine cabinet. Reaching inside, he grabbed a sterile needle and a small vial of morphine. Scurrying back to the table where Vicente lay moaning. By now, all the adrenaline had worn off. Vicente experienced every inch of pain from the trauma he had sustained from the blast.

The doctor placed his fingers on Vicente's wrist to check his heart rate. He counted sixty beats per minute. Afterward, he rolled Vicente's sleeve up, placing a blood pressure cuff around his arm. The reading was 90/65. Not great, but it would have to do.

The doctor prepared the needle, slowly pushing the metal tip into the vial. He pulled back on the plunger, drawing in a modest amount of morphine.

"This will make you feel better, Vicente. Let yourself rest." he said.

He slid the tip of the needle into Vicente's vein. Vicente turned to look at the doctor.

"When my son gets here, wake me up!"

Within a few seconds, the morphine had taken effect, and Vicente slid into unconsciousness.

Suddenly, catching everyone in the room off guard, the metal doors burst open as Ignacio charged into the room.

"Where is my father?" he blurted.

Vicente's two guards swung around, pointing their weapons at the doors, but quickly lowered them when they saw Ignacio.

The doctor stepped aside. Ignacio rushed past the two men.

"I would have already got the drop on you two fools," he huffed at them.

He saw his father on the table, unconscious, as he moved toward him. Looking at the bloody gauze on his head. He lowered his voice.

"How is he?" he asked, turning to look at the doctor.

"He is stable for now," the doctor replied calmly.

"I have only given him a tiny amount of morphine to ease his pain. I haven't examined him for other injuries."

Ignacio looked down at his father and stared at him for a moment.

"Well, get to work." he ordered.

Turning and stepping away from the table, giving the doctor room to work. Ignacio reached into his pocket to grab his phone. As he began to make a call, the metal doors once again flew open this time with Gabriella and Diego bursting into the room. Gabriella pushed passed Ignacio, not even acknowledging him, immediately rushing to Vicente's side. She ran her fingers through his blood-stained hair as her other hand grasped his.

"Mi Amor, I am here now," she whispered into his ear as he lay motionless on the table.

"What is wrong with him, doctor?" she asked as she began to tear up.

"I gave him something so he could rest. I have not done a complete examination yet; I was getting ready to do that."

Gabriella stared down at Vicente, so many thoughts racing through her mind. The strong, powerful man she loved so dearly was so weak and vulnerable right now. Who could have orchestrated such a cowardly act against their family?

"Señora De Los Santos, please allow me to start the examination," the doctor said more firmly.

"Yes, yes, of course,"

Gabriella responded, kissing Vicente on his head. She stepped away from the table, turning to Ignacio.

"Where is Lucita?"

"She's okay," Ignacio replied.

"She's outside with some guards. I told her to stay put, and you would come looking for her."

"Thank you, Ignacio," Gabriella said solemnly.

Gabriella noticed the two guards still standing in the room.

"Get out of this room while my husband is being examined!" She barked.

The two men obeyed, turning around and walking out with no response. Gabriella walked over to the doctor's desk and sat down in the chair. She leaned back, crossing her legs.

"You may proceed with your examination."

The doctor nodded and turned his attention to Vicente. He pulled back the blood-soaked gauze on Vicente's head, exposing the wound. Relieved to see that the bleeding had stopped. Repositioning the gauze, his attention turned to Vicente's knee, which was quite swollen, examining it for a range of motion.

"I will need to drain the fluid from his knee and put his kneecap back into place," he said, without turning to face Gabriella.

He grabbed a pair of large scissors from the metal tray, positioning it next to the examination table. He cut Vicente's pants leg up along the seam until the knee was exposed, seeing how severely injured it was. Going back to the white medicine cabinet, he grabbed a large needle, a bottle of rubbing alcohol, and more gauze.

"Señora De Los Santos," he said, as he walked back to the table, "you may want to look away."

Gabriella looked back at the doctor with a blank stare.

"Get on with it," she replied with coldness in her voice.

The doctor, turning his attention back to Vicente, ripped open the gauze and placed it next to him.

He poured the rubbing alcohol across the large needle to sterilize it and placed a small pillow under Vicente's knee, keeping it slightly bent. The doctor slowly advanced the large needle into Vicente's knee. Once it was halfway in, he pulled back on the large white plunger, extracting a pale fluid.

Once the syringe was full, he pulled the needle out, squirting the liquid into a small collection tray. Piercing Vicente's knee one last time, to remove any of the remaining fluid. Tossing the needle in the metal pan, the doctor continued to examine Vicente's knee, studying how disfigured it looked.

The kneecap was dislocated and needed to be put back into place. Placing his left hand under Vicente's lower leg. He grasped the knee with his right hand. Slowly he rotated Vicente's leg, rocking the patella quickly jerking his leg, popping the kneecap back into place.

Although Vicente did not wake, he let out a small moaning exhale. The doctor wrapped Vicente's leg in gauze along with a large pressure wrap around his knee. It would be enough to keep the leg stabilized until he found a more secure brace for the knee.

Now the doctor turned his attention to the gash on Vicente's head, guessing it would need seventeen stitches.

"He will not want a scar," Gabriella pointed out to the doctor.

The doctor turned and nodded. Making his way back to his medicine cabinet once again, he located a large plastic syringe and a large clear white plastic bottle.

"I'll clean and disinfect the wound first."

La Familia: Loose Ends

As he extracted the gauze back from the wound dropping it to the floor. The doctor twisted the cap from one of the large plastic bottles and poured the solution into a clean metal pan. He placed the small blunt plastic tip of the syringe into the pan, pulling back to fill the syringe. Carefully he squirted the soapy mixture along the line of the crescent-shaped wound.

After repeating the process several times until he was satisfied the wound was clean. He then grabbed a pair of tweezers from the metal tray and gently pulled back the entire flap of skin, exposing Vicente's soft tissue and the white bone of his skull. There was a considerable amount of dirt sitting inside the wound.

The doctor let the flap of skin hang open and flushed the area with the soapy mixture. Once satisfied that the injury was clean, it was time to close it. The doctor pulled a small metal rolling chair along with a bright lamp over and placed them next to the table.

As he sat down, he contemplated what it would take to properly close the gash. He selected a needle that resembled a small fishhook and the smallest thread possible. Placing his bifocals on the bridge of his nose, he proceeded to slowly thread the needle. Picking up the tweezers, he pinched a tiny piece of flesh and began stitching.

With precision and confidence, he created a beautiful pattern of seventeen small, flawless sutures. The surgical thread would dissolve on its own during the healing process. Gabriella sat in her chair, observing the doctor the whole time. She was now leaning back, smoking a cigarette.

She only smoked one kind, which her family had made especially for her; they tasted sweet and smelled like cherries. She sat back in the chair, blowing long puffs of smoke out into the room. As she took her last drag, she sat up and smashed the butt into the desk. She got up and walked out into the hallway.

"You!" she barked at one guard.

"Go and get my daughter."

The guard nodded and walked down the hallway, then up to three small steps that led to a heavy wooden door. As the door opened, he was met by the blistering heat of the day. Shielding his eyes from the sun, the guard walked into a large parking area.

Astonishing concrete statues of Aztec soldiers were placed high above, their shields and spears pointing down as symbolic gestures of eternal protection. A beautiful water fountain sat in the center of the driveway, shooting up mesmerizing displays of water mists and reflections of rainbows.

There, on the other side of the fountain, sat Lucita. She was dipping her little hand in the water, swooshing it back and forth, humming a song to herself.

"Lucita," the guard called out to her in a meek voice, "your mother wishes to see you."

Lucita looked up at him for a moment before returning her attention back to the water. It had put her into a trance-like state, carrying her far away from the chaos and murder she'd witnessed. She gazed at the crystals of water that reflected the rays of the sun.

"Lucita, please, your mother has summoned you."

Lucita removed her hand from the fountain and stood up. She walked past the guard, who trailed right behind her. Lucita walked up to the door and grabbed the metal handle, but the door was too heavy. She struggled with it. The guard reached around her, pulling the door open for her.

She walked down the three steps and into the hallway and paused, not sure which way to turn. The guard stepped around her and opened the first door on her right. Lucita hesitantly walked through the doorway and saw her mother sitting in a chair. Lucita froze when she saw the doctor sitting hunched over her father. She stared at her father, scared at how bad he looked, laying there motionless, but she was relieved to see he was alive.

"Lucita, come here, please," Gabriella said.

Lucita turned and looked at her mother, then rushed over to her, climbing into her lap.

"Mamá is Papá, okay?"

"He is fine my little one, how are you?"

Lucita shrugged her shoulders in a gesture of uncertainty,

"I am sad, I guess. My birthday party was ruined."

"Don't you worry about that right now. We will have another one, and it will be bigger and better than this one,"

Gabriella tried to reassure her, wrapping her arms around her daughter and squeezing tightly.

"Lucita, the very most important part is that you're okay."

Lucita nodded but did not smile back at her mother. Instead, she looked down at the dirty floor.

"I am hungry, can I have something to eat?" Lucita asked.

Gabriella sat there with her daughter for a moment, knowing she was not ready to process the devastation of the day.

Gabriella took in a big breath.

"Of course, you can have something to eat, my love."

She gave her daughter a kiss on the cheek. Lucita hopped down off her lap, and Gabriella stood up and held her hand. She looked at the doctor.

"I will be right outside this door," she said.

The doctor spun around in his chair and looked at her over his glasses.

"Si Señora De Los Santos."

He then spun back around to finish closing the wound on Vicente's head. Gabriella walked Lucita out the door and down a long hallway to a spiral staircase.

"I want you to go upstairs and make yourself a sandwich. When you are done, you can watch some TV. I'll be up in a little while to check on you, okay?"

Lucita looked up at the old metal staircase that wound its way up to a red door at the top.

"Will you come with me, Mamá?" she asked, feeling a sense of apprehension about making the lengthy walk by herself.

"No, I must stay with your father, but you are safe now," Gabriella said in a reassuring tone.

She knew her child was safe with the extra guards posted throughout the compound.

"You are safe here, no one can hurt us in here."

Lucita made her way up the stairs and paused at the door when she reached the top. She cracked the door open ever so slightly just before walking in.

"Is everything okay?" Gabriella asked.

"Yes, Mamá, everything is fine."

"Then go and get something to eat then."

Lucita pushed the door open and disappeared into the room. Gabriella waited for her to close the door. She stood there at the bottom of the steps for a few brief moments staring at the floor, then headed back to where Vicente was being treated.

#

Diego and Ignacio stood staring at one another in a room only a few others had knowledge of. The room was compact with two tiny windows, just barley large enough to fit the old wooden table positioned in the middle of the room. Ignacio stood at one end of the table with Diego positioned at the other. Ignacio, finally breaking his stare between them, placed his hands on the chair in front of him. He leaned over, looked down at the table and took a deep breath.

"What the hell happened?" he asked in an unsettlingly calm voice.

"I do not know what went wrong," Diego replied.

"The bomb exploded, and it was pure chaos after that."

Ignacio straightened up and began pacing from one end of the tiny room to the other. He stopped and cupped his face in his hands. He then spun around to face Diego.

"I told you only my father was to be killed—that was it! No one else in my family was to be harmed!"

He paused, a fury building within him.

"You fucking idiot! No one else in my family was to be harmed!"

Repeating the phrase, this time with anxiety and distress. With that, Ignacio whipped out one of his .45 caliber guns from his side holster, pointing it at Diego's head, cocking back the hammer. Diego froze as his eyes widened. He didn't dare breathe.

Ignacio walked toward Diego, his eyes laser-locked, his gun pointed at his head. As he got closer, Diego turned slightly to face him. Ignacio stepped close enough to press the butt of his weapon to Diego's forehead.

"My mother and my baby sister, you pendejo?" Ignacio gritted his teeth, his lips tightened as the hatred seethed out of him.

"I should fucking kill you right now!"

Diego looked helpless, unsure what Ignacio would do.

"I did exactly what you told me to do; I had the device delivered with the timer set. There was a kill switch built in to stop the bomb if the moment wasn't right. I don't know what went wrong!"

Ignacio stood silent, contemplating his next move. Every blood-thirsty, hate-filled fiber in his body wanted to pull the trigger and end this miserable failure. His finger slowly squeezing the trigger.

Still, he knew it would be impossible to explain why he had killed his best friend. Especially after Diego had just rescued his mother.

He lowered his gun and walked away from Diego, placing his weapon back in his holster. Diego let out his breath.

"Walk me through this, walk me through exactly what happened."

Diego took a big breath in.

"The white van pulled up to the front of the house as planned, exactly at 2 o'clock. The driver took the package which was gift-wrapped to look like any other children's gift and walked it back to the pool area and placed it on the table with all the other gifts. Your father was sitting at the next table. Then the driver walked back out and got in the van and took off. We had an hour before we either detonated the device or aborted the mission. We had an hour! Your father stood up from the table and walked over to the microphone with a drink in his hand and asked for everyone's attention. The band stopped playing, he started speaking about Lucita and what a special day this was for her. Then he made a toast. "

Diego paused to take another deep breath.

"Everyone raised their glasses and cheered 'Salud!' and your father went to sit down. Then the bomb detonated."

Ignacio stood there silently with his arms crossed, his back turned to Diego. He spun around quickly, speaking slowly as he stared hard at Diego.

"One of two things happened. Either the timer on the bomb wasn't set properly, or it was detonated remotely. Either way, this is fucked!" He paused for a moment.

"Here is what we will do. You are going to stay here with my mother. And most of all, you are going to keep an eye on my father!"

"Yes, Ignacio, I understand . . ."

"Shut the fuck up! I want you to stay low," Ignacio said, cutting him off, "but make sure they know you are around, and when he wakes up, you call me. I need to figure out how to clean up this mess. I'm sure my uncle is all over this by now. I have to start tying up any loose ends."

Diego knew precisely what he meant by loose ends: kill anyone who knew anything about this.

"If my mother asks where I am, you tell her I'm out starting my own investigation. And most importantly, keep your fucking mouth shut about anything else, do you hear me?"

"Yes, I understand."

Ignacio shot past Diego, exiting the secret room, leaving Diego to his thoughts. Would he be considered a loose end? Diego kept his cool for the moment, trying not to think about what might happen down the road. He needed to focus on the matter at hand, making sure that Señora De Los Santos was secure and keeping an eye on Vicente when he woke up.

Diego left the room and walked back down the long hallway. When he reached the door to where Vicente lay motionless on the table, he stuck his face in the circular window, casting a shadow on the floor. Gabriella looked over, noticing Diego standing there. She approached the door, Diego stepped back.

"Diego, what are you doing?" she asked.

"Nothing, Senora De Los Santos, just making sure everything is going okay. How do you feel?"

"I am sore, but otherwise, I am fine. Where is my son?"

"He left to start his own investigation, track down any leads," Diego responded.

"Good, whoever did this is going to pay. It will be my pleasure to stick ice picks into their eyeballs and listen to them scream and beg for mercy, beg me to let them die."

Diego made no response, but inside, terror and fear consumed him, his heart raced a hundred miles an hour.

"Why did you stay behind?" Gabriella asked.

"Don't you think you should be with my son looking for those that are responsible for this?"

"He ordered me to stay here with you and Señor De Los Santos."

"Go and make yourself useful then. Sit with Lucita. She's upstairs." she ordered.

Diego could do nothing but agree and nodded.

"Si Señora."

Gabriella watched Diego walk down the long hallway and disappear around a corner leading to the set of circular stairs. She walked back into the infirmary and stood directly behind the doctor and peered over his shoulder. He was rechecking Vicente's pulse.

"He is stable, Señora. I've done everything I can for him at the moment. He will need some time to recover from his injuries."

"Thank you, doctor. Thank you for everything you've done."

The doctor stood up from his chair. He removed his gloves, tossed them into a bin, and walked out of the room. Gabriella sat down on the small chair and took Vicente's icy hand in hers.

"Do not worry, we will find out who did this to you—who did this to us—and we'll make them pay."

As she gazed down at him, resting quietly, she thought what a luxury it was in this moment to sleep so soundly. She wondered what he was dreaming about. Gabriella understood that when Vicente awoke, he would immediately want to avenge his family's honor and take revenge against those who have perpetrated this cowardly attack against them.

She stroked her husband's salt and pepper hair, then ran her fingers through his five o'clock shadow. Gabriella was grateful he was alive, and thankful her family was alive

CHAPTER 3: Forgotten Son

"GOAL! GOAL! GOAL!" The crowd erupted; ten-thousand people filled the stadium all stood up and cheered, waving their Mexican flags. "De Los Santos! De Los Santos!"

A voice came over the loudspeaker.

"The fourth goal at forty-one minutes and twenty-eight seconds in the second half, Santino De Los Santos!"

The sun was scorching hot in the cloudless sky, and the temperature well over one-hundred degrees. However, the crowd did not care because their soccer team looked poised to win their first college championship.

Santino De Los Santos ran around the soccer field with his arms spread wide, soaring like an eagle. His teammates followed behind him, running, smiling, and jumping. All the men, laughing and hugging each other with sweat pouring down their faces.

Santino stopped in the middle of the field and bowed deeply to all four sides of the stadium as the crowd chanted his name. As he stared at the thousands of people cheering him, he soaked in the moment's glory and the joy of winning, feeling like a champion.

He then ran back to the sideline to join the rest of his teammates. His coach greeted him with an enormous smile and a congratulatory slap on the back. Santino sat down to get a well-deserved drink of ice-cold water. He squeezed the bottle tightly, forcing a long stream to shoot out.

When he finished, he doused the rest of the icy water over his head, appreciating the amazing cold sensation on his boiling hot body and sweat-soaked shirt. He gazed at the soccer field and watched as his teammates ran about kicking the ball to each other, winding the clock down to close the game out.

Santino glanced up at the clock, seeing just a few minutes left in the game, the crowd roared even louder. Men and women were waving towels above their heads and cheering. His teammates on the bench jumped up and down. Eager for the game to be over so they could claim the championship. Santino looked up at the clock again.

Only thirty seconds left, and he could taste it, not believing this day was finally here. After four long years of school, countless disappointments, and close losses, now they would be champions.

Santino sat there thinking about what a fortunate life he had, to be in this position, winning a championship when most soccer players never even got to see the playoffs. But this year, his last year in college, his last chance, he'd done it. He looked up at the clock one last time, and the countdown had begun. DIEZ, NUEVE, OCHO, SIETE, SEIS, CINCO, CUATRO, TRES, DOS, UNO . . . CERO!

They had done it, he had done it, college champions! Santino darted off the bench, running out to the middle of the field to join his teammates in what had become a hog pile of bodies, all of them screaming, "Lo Logramos! We did it!"

Grown men cried tears of happiness, joy, and jubilation. Now joining an elite class of people in history, saying something that few others could. They were the absolute best of the best. The team ran around the track of the stadium. They slapped the hands of the fans as they celebrated together, all cheering and screaming,

"Gracias, Gracias!"

Santino, the last man in the line of his teammates, walked just a bit slower now, exhausted from the game and hog pile of bodies. The women were especially happy to see Santino, and they had every reason to be.

A tall a handsome man with a full head of dark hair. He removed his shirt, exposing his impeccable six-pack abs, which were complemented by his smooth tan body and perfectly muscular physique. Every muscle flexed in his chest as he shook or slapped hands with someone. His body looked to be chiseled by God himself.

After making their way around the stadium, the two teams gathered in the center of the field for the trophy presentation. Even though the sun still battered everyone, no one was in a hurry to depart; they wanted to see their champions crowned. Eight men dressed in suits and ties walked out onto the center of the field.

Each man carried red ribbons with silver metals hanging on their right arms for the runner-up and blue ribbons with gold medals on their left arms for the champions. Two other men hauled a large silver trophy that reflected the sun's rays. It stood five feet tall with magnificent hand carvings etched all around it.

The two teams lined up on opposite sides of the field, facing one another. A loud booming voice came over the loudspeaker.

"Thank you, ladies and gentlemen, for attending today and enjoying this beautiful day of soccer." The crowd applauded.

"Both teams played with such honor and respect; it is a shame that there had to be a loser. Now we will present the ribbons to the second-place team and then the championship trophy."

As the second-place team received their medals, Santino reminisced about his life and all the obstacles he faced and overcame to make it here. He grew up in the cartel, with a family everyone feared. From his first day on campus, professors, faculty, and other students threw him looks of fear, respect, and uncertainty.

He needed to work especially hard to distance himself from the reputation they acquired—being bloodthirsty, ravenous, unforgiving, and murderous. Santino realized he grew up with a considerable amount of privilege, wealth, power, and influence.

Never did he have any misunderstandings on how his family made their billions from cocaine, marijuana and weapons. Taking a calculated risk by moving out on his own, Santino wanted to be judged for who *he* was and by *his* actions, not by his notorious family.

Santino moved away from his family the first chance that opened, knowing that he had to create as much distance as possible from them. It was dangerous not having any protection around him because people might seek revenge on him for his father's sins. However, in reality, if anyone attempted to exact revenge, it would be met by swift and deadly consequences from his father and older brother. Most certainly nobody would to take that chance.

Santino was desperate to make a life free from murder and drugs. He dreamed of running for political office and help provide the people of Mexico with clean water, food, and housing. He understood that making an actual change meant it needed to happen from the inside where the government was rotten with crooked politicians and corrupt police.

His family had been responsible for rigged elections, bribes, and having dirty cops on the De Los Santos payroll. Sadly, he came to grips with the fact that people and his country suffered because of his family. Santino looked at himself as the anti- De Los Santos. Everything he would do would be a direct contradiction to what his father stood for, destroying lives, and killing people.

Santino wanted none of that for his new life. He was taking his life in a different direction, and his family was proud of him for making it on his own like a man. Despite not joining the family business, his father seemed pleased with his son, growing up to be a man. Vicente had the best of both worlds with his two boys: Ignacio, the bull, took shit from no one, and handled business without remorse.

Santino, the brains, a thinker, college-educated and ready to start his political life.

La Familia: Loose Ends

To Vicente, concerning his sons, he could not lose. He possessed everything he needed. Muscles, brains, and power. The perfect trifecta.

Santino spoke with his mother often, sometimes two times a day. She always wanted to check up on him, ensuring he was taking care of himself and sometimes just wanting to hear his voice. He held his mother with special reverence. Even though Santino was a man, still, in some ways, he was a still a momma's boy. She protected him from Ignacio growing up.

His older brother always tried to pick a fight with him or called him weak and scared for not going into the family business. They have never developed a strong brotherly bond. Santino thought of Ignacio as a bully and a dangerous guy. Gabriella encouraged Santino to follow his passions and dreams, even if it meant making other people mad.

Santino missed his baby sister, dearly. He loved her with all of his heart, and she represented perfection to him. Her smile and the way she made him laugh, brought him utter joy. She, not yet been corrupted by the evil of the world. He loved his baby sister so profoundly that he often wondered if they crossed paths in a past life. That is how close a connection he felt with her.

Santino bowed his head for a moment, saddened he could not be there for her birthday celebration, but he knew the family would understand why. He remembered Lucita loved dolls and stuffed animals. Santino would stop by their house after the championship celebration after he'd cleaned himself up.

Santino could not wait to inform his family that they won the college soccer championship. He looked back up and saw the eight officials walking in his team's direction with their ribbons and trophy. As the men got closer, the crowd got louder. Santino's teammates waved their hands in the air, gesturing to the crowd to make more noise.

It was a remarkable sight to see a stadium full of people shouting and waving their flags to support his team. The officials made their way down the line, hanging a medal around each player's neck, shaking their hand, and congratulating them on their victory. Each player smiling from ear to ear. As they received their medal, they waved to the crowd. Finally, it was Santino's turn.

Santino bowed his head as the presenter placed a medal around his neck. "¡Felicidades! Congratulations."

"Gracias, Gracias,"

Santino replied with a gigantic smile on his face.

He held his medal in his hands, proud of his accomplishment and even happier to share at the moment with his teammates.

"And now," said the announcer over the loudspeaker,

"We would like to present this year's championship trophy to the winning team, Universidad de St. Marcos!"

With that, the entire team ran out to the center of the field where their grand trophy awaited them. Each player reaching out to place a hand on the enormous award. Some of them kissed the giant monument in a show of appreciation and gratitude. They all worked so hard to achieve this victory.

Santino gazed at the trophy, unable to find any words. Astonished that this day was here; this was his perfect moment. As Santino leaned in to kiss the trophy, he felt the ground underneath him rumble and shake just for a moment.

Oh my God, is this an earthquake? He thought.

It wasn't just Santino who felt the rumble. The players on the field, and everyone in the stands, looked around, uncertain of what to do. The crowd grew quiet. A moment later, a colossal explosion could be heard in the distance. Everyone in the stadium flinched, swinging their heads around in the direction of the blast. People sitting at the top of the stadium screamed and pointed to where they could see smoke billowing up into the sky.

Something terrible had just happened. Even though the explosion was miles away, the sheer power of the blast resonated as if it was right underneath them. A few moments later, police and fire sirens filled the air as they headed in the direction of the smoke. As Santino stared at the gray smoke rising into the air, he had no idea the blast had been an attack on his family.

<u>Chapter 4: The Bomb Maker</u>

Ignacio sat in his jet-black Lamborghini Aventador, slumped to one side in the tan leather seat. The dark-tinted windows shielded him from view. His fingers stroked his forehead, his eyes closed. Now sweating and deep in thought, he tried to envision all the details that needed to fall into place to clean up this mess and cover his ass.

Ignacio wondered how so many weeks and months of planning could go so wrong. Who else had information about the bomb besides Diego and himself? Who else had knowledge of the driver of the van? Was Diego going to keep his cool if things got hot and fell apart with his mother and father? And who made the damn bomb?

So many things to take into consideration. To top it off, Ignacio had to fix all of this, while his uncle stood neck-deep in his own investigation. Confident by now, the family's home was crawling with local and state police. He would have to stay away from there.

"The bomb maker," Ignacio said to himself.

"I need to start with him."

Not willing to take a chance on the guy talking to the police if they found him or opening his big fat mouth to anyone else who would listen.

With that, he sat up and reached over, pressing a small circular button in the middle of his console. The dashboard of the magnificent vehicle lit up, illuminating a broad spectrum of lights and displays. The engine came to life with a booming roar. Ignacio revved the gas twice, making the entire car rumble and vibrate.

Sneaking a quick peek in his rearview mirror, he stared back at himself, and then gave it a minor adjustment. Ignacio shoved the clutch down with his foot, snapping back the gear shift next to him. The tires squealed, creating a plume of white smoke around the car.

Ignacio slammed his foot down on the gas pedal and shifted the gear one more time, causing the car to take off. The vehicle twisted around one hundred and eighty degrees, shooting out of the parking area right next to the water fountain. Now Ignacio raced down the long winding drive, steering the car from one subtle turn to the next.

When he reached the end of the long road, he shot out of a small gated area and onto the main road, hooking the car violently to the right spinning his tires. As he swerved onto the gravel, the vehicle fishtailed for a moment then steadied itself on the black asphalt.

The road leading away from the De Los Santos compound traveled deep into a secluded area of the jungle. Ignacio drove along the edge of a cliff overlooking a breathtaking view. Mist rose above the tops of brilliant green jungle trees. The sun had set, dark cloud formations rolled in from a distance, signaling a nasty storm.

Ignacio interpreted the dark clouds as a sign of the bleak times ahead and how he would navigate. How fitting, he thought to himself.

Violence and chaos never seemed to be a stranger to him; he grew up in them, committing his first murder at the age of thirteen. Extortion, robbery, kidnapping, beheading people, you name it Ignacio had done it. This was different. However, he had ordered a hit on his father, the king, and missed!

Ignacio had an extreme appreciation for the gravity of the situation, that once his father awoke, he would not stop searching until he found the person or persons responsible for this. Ignacio had no misgivings that his father would leave no rock unturned. He would travel to the ends of the earth and spend any amount of money it took to flush out the cowards that came at him.

In his mind, Ignacio feared no man on the planet, no man that is but his father. A man regarded by all in Mexico as the most vicious, savage, ruthless, sadistic, cruel human being walking the face of the planet. The things he had seen his father do to other people over the years gave even Ignacio room to pause.

He flashed back to the time when he was fourteen. A couple who worked for his father were caught stealing money from him. When brought to his attention, Vicente went crazy demanding they be delivered to him. He placed each one of them in a barrel of oil and made each of them beg for their lives for three days.

While still tied up, Vicente made small cuts on their bodies with a rusty knife, laughing and smoking his cigar. Finally, on the third day, tired of listening to them beg, he stood up and threw his lit cigar into the barrel with the woman. Vicente forced the man to watch as his wife screamed and burned to death right in front of him.

After she died, Vicente kicked the barrel over, spilling her body out onto the concrete. The man sat in his barrel of oil for a day, an entire twenty-four hours, with his wife's corpse laying there right in front of him. He had to smell her rotting flesh and look at her charred remains. The next morning Vicente sat and ate breakfast in front of the man and conducted business on the phone.

When he finished, he decapitated the man and then set his body on fire. Afterward, Vicente had Ignacio place both of their bodies in the middle of the city; in a kids' park, as an example to everyone that you never EVER cross the De Los Santos family.

Ignacio snapped himself out of this memory. He wondered if his father would have the heart to do that to him, his own flesh and blood. Simply put, hell yes, but it would be much, much worse. His wife and daughter had been hurt; this was a no brainer. Ignacio knew he would be made to suffer.

Physically, he could probably beat his father in a fight. Still, he wouldn't stand a chance against his father's worldwide network of mercenaries and assassins. Ignacio would have to be smarter and quicker than his father, always one step ahead to weather this storm.

When he reached the bottom of the mountain road, he slowed down. The last thing he needed was to get pulled over for speeding.

La Familia: Loose Ends

The skies thundered as the clouds rolled in. Deep rolling booms and wicked rumbles filled the air. The rain trickled down slowly, eventually opening up into a full down pour. People in the streets made their way inside. Ignacio traveled along neighborhood roads, making a series of left and right turns.

After navigating out of the residential area, he drove down to a semi-remote location of abandoned houses, warehouses, and factories. The roads had now become muddy from the rain. Taking his time to examine all the run-down shacks. One house, in particular, caught his eye.

A standalone building sitting right next to a warehouse. It had a tremendous number of antennas on the roof. Communication antennas, TV antennas, radio antennas, yup, this was his guy, THE BOMB MAKER! Ignacio had told Diego to use his connections to facilitate the details around the making of the bomb. He wanted to distance himself from it.

Looking back now, Ignacio realized what a dumb move that was. He should have been involved from day one, to help directly oversee every detail, but now he put himself at a disadvantage. Unaware of this person's identity. Ignacio pulled over and parked at a distance to get a good look at the building.

He sat there for a few minutes, just staring at it. The building, dirty white with chipped paint. Long streaks of old rust cascaded down the side, three levels with two windows on every floor. No movement going in or coming out of the building, thick steel bars on all the windows. It looked like a fortress.

The small warehouse next to the building had no windows abandoned mostly. Ignacio wondered what the smartest play was here. Should he just walk right up to the front door and knock? Should he call for some of his men to come and back him up?

No, that would only get more people involved than he wanted. Then he remembered one crucial thing. Ignacio De Los Santos did not need backup from anyone. Ignacio pulled the latch on the driver's side door, releasing the lock. He waited as the hydraulic door lifted. Ignacio stepped out and swung the door back down, securing it shut.

Despite the rain, a few people remained on the street. They stopped and stared with fierce curiosity who this stranger was in the outrageously expensive vehicle. When the people finally realized Ignacio De Los Santos stood in front of them, they couldn't believe their eyes. They became shocked and terrified. "El Diablo," the devil himself stood before them.

The remaining women grabbed their children by the hand and quickly hurried them inside their homes. Men sitting in front of the small food market got up and started walking away in different directions, just to get away as quickly. Ignacio watched their reactions, realizing the neighborhood understood exactly who he was.

Ignacio stepped away from his vehicle and started walking toward the building. Despite being in the slums, Ignacio exuded a stench of confidence that nobody would dare mess with him. He didn't even bother locking his car. When he reached the front door of the building, he attempted to peer through a window.

Seeing nothing through the dirty screen and the white drape that partially obscured the view inside. He pounded on the old wooden door with the sizeable meaty part of his fist, with no answer. Ignacio slammed his fist against the door three more times. Eventually hearing a man's voice calling out,

"Announce yourself, who are you?"

Ignacio looked all around but saw no one.

"Announce yourself," the voice repeated.

"Who are you? Look up at the camera!"

Ignacio looked up above his right shoulder to a small camera with a red flashing light.

Staring directly up at the camera, he said calmly and with a slight hint of arrogance,

"Do I REALLY have to tell *YOU* who *I* am?"

With that the door in front of him buzzed and slightly popped open. Ignacio pushed the door open with his foot, exposing a high set of steps leading up to a dark hallway. He grabbed his gun from his holster and slid back the chamber to make sure he had a bullet ready to fly if needed.

Looking down at the ground, Ignacio saw a tiny rock on the ground and placed it between the door and the base of the door jamb to prevent it from latching shut. He walked in and stood at the base of the stairwell, positioning his body to the left side. El Diablo clasped his gun with both hands, pointing it up toward the top of the staircase.

His senses now in a hyper state of awareness. Ignacio noticed the heavy smell of chemicals in the building. Giving him a familiar feel. Gasoline, ether, plastic explosives, all the ingredients needed to make a nasty bomb. He had no doubts he was definitely in the right place. His reflexes extra sharp, he would not let anyone get the drop on him.

Ignacio wouldn't hesitate to unload the entire clip if needed. Slowly starting to creep up the steps, his eyes locked down the iron sights of his pistol. Ignacio pressed his body and shoulder so tight to the wall it left a streak of white residue on his black shirt.

He carefully advanced up the stairs, each footstep slow and precise. Ignacio stopped short of the last three steps; not ready to break the plane of the hallway just yet. He peered around the corner slowly, seeing nothing but darkness. He hurried to the other side of the staircase, slamming his body into the wall, his gun still pointed straight in front of him.

This time he moved up one more step, staying very low as he peered down the opposite side of the hallway. Still nothing but darkness. Ignacio climbed the last two steps, finally breaching into the hallway. He snapped his body around to get a quick look at the other side, there was nothing but emptiness.

As his eyes adjusted to the dark, he noticed a small glimmering light under a door. He could faintly hear the sounds of a television coming from behind it. He locked all of his attention on the door as he started walking toward it, pressing his body along the wall. When he reached the door, he gently placed his ear up against the door, listening for any movement from inside the room, everything seemed quiet.

He reached down and attempted to turn the doorknob, but the door was locked.

"Open the door!" he called out.

He looked down at the floor, seeing a figure casting a shadow in front of the light. He carefully took a step back and raised his gun.

"Open the door! I won't ask again!" he demanded.

He heard a series of locks being manipulated on the other side of the door, then a sliding chain. The doorknob turned slowly, and the door cracked open. Ignacio rushed the door like a mad bull, forcing his full body weight into the door, leading with his shoulder. The force of the impact made the door split slightly in the middle.

As Ignacio forced his way into the room, the door hit the mysterious middle-aged man, causing him to stumble backward into a cabinet. Ignacio, now entirely inside the apartment, stood there, glaring at him. He had his gun trained on him as he fell to the floor. The man had sustained a minor cut on his head from the impact of the door, a slight trickle of blood dripped from the top of his hairline.

"Do you know who I am?" Ignacio asked.

The man looked up at him with a pained expression.

"I asked you a question. Do you know who I am?"

"Yes, you are El Diablo!"

Ignacio used his foot to shut the door behind him, never breaking eye contact with the man.

"If you know who I am, then you know what I will do to you if you look at me wrong, don't you?"

The man sat up. "Yes, I am aware."

Ignacio put his gun in his holster. He stepped forward, grabbing the man by his shirt collar, pulling him up, slamming him once again back into the stack of cabinets.

"Fucking stand there and don't move!" he ordered.

"Is there anyone else in here with you?"

"No."

"Don't fucking lie to me!" Ignacio snapped back.

"I am not lying. I live here and work here alone."

Ignacio spun the bomb maker around, now standing directly behind him. Using him as a shield, he walked him into the living room area. He pulled his gun once again just in case he needed to let off a few rounds.

"Nice and slow asshole,"

Ignacio whispered as he led him forward. He peered over the man's shoulders as they walked forward together. As they reached the living room, Ignacio quickly thrust his gun over the shoulder of the bomb maker and scanned the room.

The room looked dingy, with minimal lighting along with severely tattered hand-me-down furniture that smelled wet and damp. On the other hand, he was impressed with what he saw.

One hundred cases of C-4, thousands of sticks of dynamite, remote glass detonators, ten drums of gasoline (each holding fifty-five gallons), radio communication devices, what looked like hundreds of cell phones, boxes of clocks, and seven state-of-the-art televisions all playing different news channels, and some not-so-impressive furniture.

By now, news of the explosion at his family's home had spread, and reporters were live from the residence. Ignacio eyeballed one of the TVs for a quick moment, as a female reporter stood at the scene.

"Here, sit."

Ignacio barked as he threw the bomb maker down on a couch.

He walked backward, never looking away from the bomb maker until he reached a small table. He grabbed the remote and turned the volume down on the television.

"You were given a job a few months ago from an associate of mine. You built a bomb, but it went off too soon. I'm here to figure out why. You're going to tell me everything that you put in the bomb and what made it go off at the wrong time."

The bomb maker looked back with fear in his eyes.

"Señor, please, I mean no disrespect, but you are going to have to be more specific. I make lots of bombs for people." tears started to swell.

With his gun, Ignacio pointed to the female reporter on the television screen,

"A bomb wrapped inside a child's present." Ignacio said.

"Oh yes, I know which one you are speaking about. That was your house, what went wrong with it?"

With that question, Ignacio charged over to the bomb maker and slammed his hand against the wall directly beside his head.

"I am asking the fucking questions pendejo, and THAT is what I want to know. Why the fuck did it go off unexpectedly?"

Ignacio was mere inches from the man's face, the bomb maker was too terrified to look at him turning his head and closing his eyes. He slid back as far into the couch as his body would let him.

His breathing was heavy, he panted, the sweat and blood from his cut were now running into his right eye.

Ignacio stood back up, sauntering around the room, glancing at his surroundings. He spun around to sit on a stool next to the table.

"I don't have a lot of time, so this is how it will go. I will ask you questions. You tell me the truth, and I will not hurt you. If you lie to me, then you will suffer more than you can imagine.

"Understand?"

The bomb maker nodded.

"When my associate approached you about making this device, what did he tell you it was for?"

"Señor, he did not tell me what it was for. He just said he needed a bomb and that it had to be wrapped like a child's present. That was it, I swear to you!"

Ignacio peered at the man, squinting his eyes.

"And you were okay with making a bomb for a child's party?" Even though Ignacio was not in any proper position to be a moral authority.

"Señor, in my line of work, I do not ask questions, I just do as I'm told, and for the amount of money he was paying me, I did not wish to pry."

"How much did he pay you, and how?"

"He paid me two million pesos, all in cash."

"What sort of explosive material did you use?"

Ignacio took a quick glance down at his watch to keep track of the time.

"I used a mercury switch with a bimetallic strip, a simple battery, and some nitroglycerin."

"Wait, what? Say that again?"

Ignacio sat up at complete attention.

"I used a mercury switch with a simple battery and nitroglycerin."

The bomb maker's second response sounded confused, his voice was high pitched, he appeared to be in even more distress.

"You did not use a timer? Did my associate tell you to use a timer?"

Ignacio slamming his fist in the counter, demanding answers.

"Yes, he did, he also said he needed something with a kill switch, but that didn't allow me to put a timer in it."

Ignacio sat in a stunned state of disbelief, it made sense why the bomb might have gone off early. If the bomb maker used a mercury switch and nitroglycerin, then even a slight bump to the table could have triggered the bomb.

Or just the searing heat from the day could have made it explode prematurely. Still, he hadn't followed the instructions. Diego was also sloppy for not ensuring it was exactly what he ordered the man to make.

"So, let me get this straight. First, you used a highly volatile substance on a scorching hot day. Second, you were told to make a bomb with a timer AND a kill switch, but you didn't. Third, you decided to go off and make what you wanted?"

Ignacio was now leaning on the counter where he sat, with his gun pointed at the bomb maker.

"Did it not occur to you to contact my associate and tell him it could not be done instead of just making what you wanted? Are you aware it almost killed my mother and baby sister today? Because of your shitty excuse for a bomb. They would have been in a safe area by the time the bomb was supposed to go off."

The bomb maker sat in terror, staring into Ignacio's eyes, his forehead sweating profusely.

"Please, Señor, I did the best I could. I had no clue it was for you or your family. Please, I know nothing. I will tell no one!"

La Familia: Loose Ends

By now, the bomb maker was in full panic mode, fearing for his life. He was sitting on the couch facing Ignacio with his arms held out; his hands clasped together, tears running down his face. He shuffled to the edge of the sofa, slumping onto the floor, crawling on his hands and knees toward Ignacio.

When he reached Ignacio's black snakeskin cowboy boots, he kneeled down, placing his hands and face on them.

"Please, Señor, I beg of you, I would say nothing to no one, not the police . . . not anyone!"

Ignacio stood up with the bomb maker sobbing at his feet. He reached into a small compartment on the side of his holster, pulling out a small cylinder-shaped object and screwed it into the barrel of his gun. Ignacio stared down, unfazed by the man crying at his feet. Ignacio made one last adjustment to the silencer.

The bomb maker sat up and looked up at Ignacio. He knew there was nothing more to be said. His eyes glazed over, he began whispering a prayer, making peace with his God. Ignacio walked behind the man who now stared straight ahead at a picture of Jesus Christ hanging on the wall.

After a moment, the bomb maker was now devoid of all emotion. Ignacio pressed the black silencer to the back of the bomb maker's head, and with a gentle squeeze of the trigger, it was over. The man's body fell dead to the floor as a large spray of skull fragments and brain matter were sent flying across the room. The last thing the bomb maker heard was the soft whisper of the gun.

Ignacio wasted no time and did not stop to think about what he had just done. He needed to make sure all evidence of his presence was gone. Although he was no bomb maker, he knew enough to make a basic explosive. He looked around the room and found what he needed.

Corey Cepeda

A large drum of gasoline and six sticks of dynamite with a twenty-foot fuse would do the trick. He taped the dynamite to the side of the fifty-five-gallon barrel and then fashioned a long enough fuse to trail out of the apartment and into the hallway.

As he was leaving the apartment, Ignacio took one last glance at the television on the wall. He saw the female reporter now speaking with his uncle, Aurelio. The TV was muted, but he already understood the gist of the report; his uncle was heading the case. That meant Ignacio had to get to people fast before his uncle did.

Aurelio was smart, and a powerful policeman, and would piece this thing together quickly. Ignacio finished trailing the fuse out of the apartment. When he reached the top of the staircase, he dropped the long fuse to the floor, reaching into his pocket and pulling out his lighter. He took one last look down the hallway and lit the fuse.

Ignacio sprinted down the long flight of steps, balancing himself with his left arm against the wall. As he darted out the door, he began speed walking to his car, knowing the device he'd made would blow big at any moment. The street was still clear. The rain by now was falling like a monsoon. He reached his car and pulled back the handle.

As the car door swung up, he jumped in, pulling the door back down while simultaneously pressing the ignition button. The engine fired up along with the dash board. Ignacio shifted into gear, slamming his foot down on the gas. Just as he was speeding away, the sky lit up with a bright red fireball.

He looked into his rearview mirror, seeing the building explode in devastating fashion. The ground shook beneath him from the concussion of the explosion.

The incredible force of the detonation blew out the top floor first, then caused the rest of the building to explode in a brilliant configuration of blue, green, and red flames. All the chemicals in that apartment were reacting in quick succession.

La Familia: Loose Ends

Ignacio knew he had attracted attention, but most people would figure the explosion occurred because of all the chemicals in the apartment. And anyone who had seen him there wouldn't have the balls to rat him out. He drove away feeling like he had closed one loop; the bomb maker was dead.

There would be nothing left but rubble. Ignacio now shifted his mind to the next phase of his clean up; taking care of another loose end.

Chapter 5: The Van Driver

Ignacio drove off into the night, his headlights illuminated the muddy road in front of him. He realized that he had not checked in with Diego in quite some time and needed an update on how his fathers' condition. If he was lucky enough, his father might have succumbed to his injuries, which would mean he would now assume the family empire.

He also needed to know if his mother had been asking questions. Before he placed a call to Diego, he needed to make sure he had enough distance between him and the mess he just left behind. Ignacio knew the local police would already be swarming to the explosion.

For obvious reasons, he did not need to be spotted anywhere near it. As he drove out of the nearby residential area and found his way onto a major highway. He opened up the finely tuned engine, taking off like a lightning bolt.

Ignacio pressed a button on the steering wheel, turning the radio on. It was perfect timing as his favorite rapper Kendrick Lamar had started playing. Ignacio's adrenaline was jacked and he needed to release some energy. As the luxury sports vehicle tore down the open highway, he cranked the volume up and blasted *HUMBLE*.

He reached a blazing speed of 160 miles an hour, weaving his way in and out of traffic. He flashed by too fast for anyone on the road to make out details of who had been driving. Gripping the steering wheel with both hands so tight his knuckles turned a shade of white. As he gained even higher speed, the highway lights looked like white dots shooting past him.

He stared through the windshield with intense focus, every car around him becoming a blur as he passed by them. All they would see would be a jet-black car with tinted windows.

La Familia: Loose Ends

After putting fifty miles between him and the explosion, Ignacio slowed down. He decided to take an exit ramp that led him to a stretch of road that ran parallel to the ocean. The night sky perfectly beautiful, with mesmerizing display of lightning strikes throughout the clouds.

Each time the lightning struck, it lit up the ocean, exposing the waves crashing onto the beach. The rain had all but stopped at this point. Ignacio rolled down his window and let the cool breeze from the salty ocean air move through his car. He pulled over and parked alongside a small embankment before turning the car off and stepping out.

Ignacio walked across the two-way road and stopped at a huge wire barrier that served as a protective guard for vehicles. Staring out at the surf, he enjoyed the rare moment of silence and peace. While standing there, Ignacio wondered how he'd gotten to this point. How could he let this get so sloppy?

He should have taken care of this himself and never allowed Diego to handle the hit on his father alone. But none-the-less he was here now, and there was no time to bitch and moan about it.

He pulled out his cell phone and auto dialed Diego's number. After three rings, Diego picked up.

"Ignacio, where are you, is everything okay?"

Ignacio could tell that Diego was attempting to whisper while trying to make it appear like he was having a normal conversation. He must be near Gabriella or Vicente, Ignacio thought.

"How is my father doing?"

"Your father is fine, he is resting. Your mother has been with him this whole time. She hasn't left the room once. I have been with your sister, watching over her this entire time."

"So, you have heard nothing? My mother hasn't been asking any questions?"

"No." Diego replied.

Maybe he still had time to get ahead of this. Ignacio thought.

"And my father is he awake yet?"

"No, he is still sleeping."

"Tell me about the driver of the van. Who is he?"

Ignacio's voice shifted, becoming stern.

"He is a young kid off the streets, early twenties," Diego replied. "He wanted to make some extra cash and wanted to get into our good graces, so I hired him."

"Did you tell him who he would be working for?" Ignacio asked, hoping that Diego had not been reckless enough to drop his name.

"No, I didn't say it for you specifically, but this kid knows that I work for you, so he probably put the rest together."

"What did you tell him? ... SPECIFICALLY!"

Ignacio snapped back.

"I told him I needed someone to drive a van for me to a birthday party and deliver a child's present. That's it. I would get back to him with a date and time to do the job."

"You never mentioned that there would be a bomb inside or where he would deliver it to?"

"Absolutely not. I'm not that dumb."

Ignacio rolled his eyes.

"How much did you pay him?"

"I told him he would get ninety-three thousand pesos if he did exactly what I said. I would pay him half before the job, and the rest after he completed delivery."

Ignacio stood silent for a moment, thinking.

"Where did the van come from?"

"From one of your chop shops. All the serial numbers and vehicle identification numbers we removed and ground off. I made sure it was clean before I . . ."

Ignacio interrupted,

"Wait, you used a van from one of my businesses, you asshole? Is that what you just fucking told me?"

Ignacio's eyes squeezed shut as he pinched the bridge of his nose,

"You couldn't have gone out and stolen a van and switched license plates. You used a van that anyone might have seen coming out of my shop."

Ignacio now seethed with anger.

"Ignacio, I swear to you the van was clean before I gave it to him. I made sure of it."

What an absolute idiot, Ignacio thought. Diego had not only picked a shitty bomb maker but now had also potentially linked him to the attack. If his uncle could tie that van to his shop, it would be catastrophic. He stood there staring out at the ocean, gazing as far as his eyes would let him.

A small cluster of clouds parted, exposing the bright full moon. The moonlight shining down on the black water gave it a sinister look.

"What's the guy's name?" Ignacio asked coldly.

"Ruben. He hangs out over by the main strip in the plaza."

"Give me a description?"

"Younger kid, bald, short, tattoos all over his body, one on his right hand, a skull and crossbones. Goes by the street name Jaguar."

Without saying goodbye, Ignacio hung up the phone. Diego had now made his second mistake. How could he be so sloppy with the stakes so high? It became clear that Diego had not made sound decisions. He would have to deal with him later. He had to get to this kid, Ruben.

Ignacio crossed back over the road and climbed into his vehicle. He knew what strip Diego spoke of. Located not too far outside of

Mazatlán, in Sinaloa where most of the street kids hung out to sell drugs, rob people, party, or cause trouble.

As Ignacio took off, he started thinking about the best method for locating this kid. It wasn't like he had a door to walk up to; it was attempting to find a needle in a haystack.

Ignacio sped down the road, arriving at a T in the intersection. Making a sharp right turn and driving another five miles, he finally arrived at the strip. The streets were alive with tons of action, young teenagers and adults walking around from one nightclub to another.

Each club blasted a different music: techno, salsa, rap, reggae; everything looked to be one big party. Food vendors pushed carts, selling tacos to feed the appetites of tired and intoxicated bodies as they made their way through the streets. Ignacio immediately realized how much more difficult the sea of bodies made it for him than he had initially thought.

As he drove slowly down the strip, he rolled down both windows to get a better view of the crowds. He moved his head from right to left, scanning everyone, hoping to get lucky. A small group of teenagers to his left caught his attention. One guy, in particular, stood out, laughing more obnoxiously, more animated than the rest. He fit Jaguar's description perfectly.

Short, bald head, gray muscle shirt, long black pants with a matching black cargo jacket, a few gold chains, and tattoos all over his upper body. Ignacio couldn't tell if he had the skull and crossbones tattooed on his right hand. Still, he couldn't allow this opportunity to pass him by without checking it out.

Making a sharp left turn, he pulled into an alleyway parking next to the nightclub. As he exited his vehicle, he removed his gun from his leather holster, tossing the holster inside the car. He drew back the slide of his gun slightly, looking down the inner barrel to make sure he had a bullet in the chamber. Tucking the gun in the back of his pants, he pulled down the car door and locked his vehicle.

La Familia: Loose Ends

Ignacio walked around to the front of the building, making mental notes of everything. Aware of his surroundings, as his father had taught him growing up; you never let your guard down. As he approached the front entrance, a long line of people waited to enter.

Ignacio walked confidently to the front of the line, not making eye contact with anyone. He didn't need to, because they were nobodies to him. Two rather huge, beefy bouncers dressed in all black business attire, wearing dark sunglasses, positioned themselves blocking the entrance to the door.

They were not muscular, but they both took up a lot of space. Ignacio pushed his way forward, causing people to shoot him dirty looks. Now standing directly in front of both bouncers, Ignacio reached into his front pocket, pulling out a massive wad of cash.

Thumbing off a few large bills, he folded them in half and placed them between his fingers. Without saying anything, he extended his hand. One of the bouncers shook his head and waved his finger at Ignacio.

"Your money is no good here, Mr. De Los Santos, you can go right in."

The crowd moaned, but Ignacio ignored the rumble. He had other matters to attend to.

As he entered the building, the music was deafening, Ignacio needed to take a few seconds to let his eyes adjust to the dark environment. The loud bass from the techno music made the air shake and vibrate all around him.

The hallway was lit with black lights, which made everyone's dark clothes light up in ultraviolet color. Women engaged in conversations, standing around in the hallway, sipping their drinks as they noticed the handsome Ignacio standing there.

They threw beautiful smiles and sexy looks at him. However, Ignacio now in full hunt mode and would not be distracted. He walked by them to an opening, walking through a black dangling drape that led to the dance floor.

Strobe lights, flashing party lights, and manmade fog filled the room. Hundreds of people consumed the dance floor with glow sticks wrapped around their necks and waving them above their heads. Ignacio saw people taking hits of LSD and other nefarious drugs, more than likely sold by his family.

He made his way slowly around the dance floor, attempting to look at every single face out there, bodies continuously bumping into him. On any other given night, if someone had bumped into Ignacio without apologizing, there would have been severe, if not deadly repercussions.

Still, tonight he needed to be laser-focused, and these unknowing people would get a pass. The large stage where the DJ blasted his music was crowded. For Ignacio, definitely not an ideal setting. Ignacio stopped at the bar, finding a small opening to lean back against.

The flashing lights, all the movement—just the sheer volume of bodies alone made it impossible to make out faces. He needed to take a few minutes to survey the land. A voice started yelling at him above the music.

"What will you have?"

Ignacio turned around and saw a gorgeous woman working at the bar. She stood there staring at him, waiting for his response.

"What do you want?" she asked again.

"I'll have a shot of Patrón, with a chaser."

The bartender walked away to grab his drinks. Ignacio watched her, admiring her shape. He reached into his pocket and pulled out his bundle of money once again.

When the bartender returned with his shot and beer chaser, he grabbed her hand. He ogled her, sending an obvious message that he thought she was beautiful. Ignacio leaned in, while still gripping her hand, his face close to hers. Ignacio handed her one hundred pesos and yelled,

"You can keep the change."

She smiled, biting her lower lip, he released her hand. She walked down to the end of the bar to continue working.

Ignacio downed his shot of tequila, followed quickly by his chaser, slamming both glasses down on the bar. He spun back around; looking at the dance floor, realizing a whole second level to this massive club existed. Ignacio walked away from the bar and made his way to a staircase, but it was roped off and reserved for a VIP crowd.

Once again, another huge man wearing dark sunglasses stood at the entrance. Ignacio walked up to the bouncer, but he wasn't as keen to let him pass through. The guy stood there, attempting to look menacing.

Ignacio looked at the man and shouted,

"I'm looking for a younger guy, tattoos all over his upper body, with a skull and crossbones on his right hand. Goes by the name Jaguar. Sound familiar?"

The bouncer stood there for a second, looked Ignacio up and down, and nodded.

"Yeah, he and his crew went up a few minutes ago, but no one gets up there unless they're on the list."

"I need to speak to him," Ignacio replied.

Suddenly, the bouncer placed his finger on his earpiece. He paused briefly, taking a step back.

"My deepest apologies, Mr. De Los Santos. I didn't recognize you. Of course, you are free to go up."

Clearly, someone in the nightclub had made the announcement to all the bouncers that "El Diablo" was in the building. The tone in the bouncer's voice had a twinge of *oh shit* in it as he realized he tried to be a badass to the ultimate badass, and it easily could have cost him his life.

"Maybe if you take off your dark sunglasses, you could see something," Ignacio replied dryly.

"Of course, Mr. De Los Santos."

With a slight tremble in his hands, the bouncer removed his glasses. He unhooked the tethered rope and stepped to the side, allowing Ignacio to make his way up the red-carpeted staircase. When Ignacio reached the top, he looked around momentarily. As he glanced to his left, he saw exactly who he was looking for.

There sat Jaguar at the very back in a booth with several others surrounding him. Ignacio started sizing him up along with the others around the table, making mental notes of the exits and quickly scanning the room for any potential dangers. Jaguar had an average build, possibly a bit smaller than Ignacio.

He was sitting in the middle of a curved booth, which was a good thing for Ignacio; Jaguar wouldn't be able to get away quickly if things went south. The rest of his crew looked to be around the same age. A few guys and girls, no one he feared physically. Still, nonetheless, he had to take them into consideration as a threat.

The music was even louder on the second level. The speakers suspended above the DJ's area pointed directly at the balcony, and they were enormous. Ignacio thought this could work to his advantage. If he got into a gunfight, no one would necessarily notice.

However, there wasn't much of a crowd in the VIP area, so if something went down, he wouldn't have the advantage of using human shields. The best course of action would be to remove Jaguar from the club. That would separate him from all the eyes and ears of potential witnesses.

Ignacio started moving toward the booth where Jaguar sat. As he got closer, it was obvious that everyone at the table was drunk or high. Clearly under the influence of something. Empty bottles of champagne littered the table along with burned-out stubs of marijuana.

They were a young, loud, and obnoxious crew, laughing and screaming at each other. Two teenage girls danced at the front of the table when Ignacio walked up behind them, nudging them out of his way. They turned and looked to see who had just butted their way in between them. Their eyes grew big as they realized who stood in their presence.

They quickly stepped to the side, saying nothing. The volume and pace of the techno music seemed to amplify their sense of anxiousness. Ignacio stood in front of the table, staring directly at Jaguar, who hadn't yet noticed El Diablo in his presence. Jaguar's face, along with his full attention, were both immersed in the neck of a sweet young lady that giggled intensely.

Ignacio stood there eyeballing this punk oblivious to the world around him. Finally, the young female stopped laughing when she looked up and noticed Ignacio standing there. She quickly sat up and gave Jaguar a hard nudge. Jaguar sat up, looking at her, and then turned to see Ignacio standing in front of him.

He cocked his head, acknowledging that evil was standing just inches from him.

"Oh shit, I can't believe it's you! Ignacio! You fools see this?" Jaguar said, turning to look at the others around him.

"I have the MAN standing in front of me!"

Ignacio stood still, an icy glare developing in his eyes as he considered what he should do with this young punk kid.

"Only my family calls me Ignacio, my associates call me Mr. De Los Santos. You are neither, so you should sit there and be quiet for the moment." Ignacio's face was expressionless. His words were ice cold.

Jaguar sat there, unresponsive for a moment.

"That's cool man . . . I mean, Mr. De Los Santos. Oh, shit. I mean . . . I don't know what I mean."

He started to quickly sober up and become a little flustered.

"I need to speak with you in private. Tell your guests it's time to go."

"You fools heard the man. Get the fuck out of here. He needs to speak with me about business and shit." Jaguar barked.

The group got out of the booth as Ignacio stood there in front of the table. Never breaking his hard stare at Jaguar. The girl Jaguar had been making out with slid her way out of the booth.

She looked nervous and being extra cautious as she attempted to stand up so she wouldn't bump into or touch Ignacio. She glanced back at Jaguar one last time with a look of uncertainty.

"Hurry the fuck up!"

Jaguar screamed at her. She jumped out of the booth, shuffled off to the staircase and headed down to the main floor. Ignacio walked around the table, sitting down on the edge of the booth. Jaguar tried to look in control and relaxed however on the inside, his heart raced as he knew was no match for Ignacio.

Jaguar sat back in the booth, opened his arms as wide as they would go, laying them across the back of the headrest.

"So, I guess you're here to offer me a job finally, huh?" he said smugly.

What arrogance, Ignacio thought. How brazen and ignorant is this fool? His head now hurting from the pounding music.

"And why exactly would I do that?" he countered.

"Because of the outstanding job I did for you. You know—driving that van and shit."

Ignacio's face broke into a smirk; he was done with this kid and his smart-ass attitude. He was done with this conversation. Everything in Ignacio's body screamed that he wanted to kill this arrogant punk right here and now, but even by his own standards, that would be sloppy.

Then an idea suddenly hit him like a lightning bolt. Ignacio relaxed his posture and leaned back in the booth. He pointed at Jaguar and smiled,

"You're a smart kid, and you have huge balls. That job you did for me *was* perfect." He paused a moment.

"So, you're right, I am here to offer you another job."

Jaguar let out a big breath.

"Holy shit, Mr. De Los Santos, if I can call you that. You had me scared. I hate to admit fear, but I'm glad to hear you say that."

Jaguar let out a nervous laugh, then grabbed a bottle of champagne sitting in front of him and took a big gulp. He slammed the bottle back down on the table and wiped his face with his sleeve.

"Whatever you need me to do, I'm your guy. You need me to smoke some fools, I'll do it!"

Ignacio chuckled.

"One small step at a time. Actually, I need another delivery, but this time its product. Can you drive for me again?"

Jaguar sat there feeling like he had hit the jackpot. It was his time to finally shine and become someone in the De Los Santos army.

"Sure, I can. Sure, I can do that for you. Just tell me where and when."

"Tonight, right now. One of my drivers got picked up by the police, so I'm a driver short."

Ignacio paused. "Two-hundred kilos of powder, but I need a driver right now. You in?"

Jaguar should have known one thing about the De Los Santos family: the police did not arrest soldiers from the De Los Santos crew. Most of them were paid well to turn their heads.

Something his Uncle Aurelio battled every day. However, without hesitation or thought, Jaguar pounded both fists on the table.

"Fuck yeah!" he yelled, loud enough that Ignacio had to motion to him to quiet down.

"Good. We need to go now. I'm already running behind." Ignacio said.

Ignacio stood up, sliding himself out of the booth. Jaguar slid out from the other side and stumbled as he attempted to stand, clearly too intoxicated to drive any vehicle. Still, all Jaguar could think about was his opportunity with El Diablo.

Jaguar started walking and stumbling toward the staircase as Ignacio walked behind him, not noticing the devilish grin on Ignacio's face. How stupid and gullible is this kid? Ignacio wondered. This was perfect, way too easy, getting this punk out of the nightclub. It didn't require guns or violence, just pure manipulation.

It was the best-case scenario. They made their way down the staircase. When they reached the bottom, the large bouncer once again unhooked the rope allowing both men to pass through. As Ignacio and Jaguar made their way through the club, Jaguar slowed down, turning around to face Ignacio.

"Where are we going?"

Ignacio leaned into Jaguar's shoulder to talk over the music.

"To my car. I'm parked on the side of the building."

As they weaved their way through the last section of the dance floor, Jaguar made eye contact with the young girl that he had been making out with. She was standing at the bar with the other members of his crew, waiting anxiously for a small sign. Jaguar's face broke out into a smile as he looked at her. His expression was one of excitement and anticipation.

She looked back at him with a slight twinge of angst, but if he was giving her the all-clear gesture, then everything had to be okay.

"I'll be back," he mouthed to her. With that, the two proceeded down the hallway and out the front door.

Finally, Ignacio was free from the hammering beat of the music. He and Jaguar stepped out onto the sidewalk.

"Over here to the left," Ignacio said, guiding Jaguar toward his car.

As they reached the corner and turned into the alley, Jaguar laid eyes on Ignacio's car.

"Oh, snap. This your ride?"

"Of course it is. What do you think?" Ignacio replied.

The growing tone of aggravation in his voice had become more difficult to control.

"Watch your feet getting in, don't scratch my car."

Ignacio pulled out his keys and unlocked the car door. When the door swung up, Jaguar looked on in disbelief. He had only dreamed of being this close to such a magnificent vehicle, let alone actually getting into one.

"Pull the handle," Ignacio said. Jaguar looked at him with a complete look of confusion on his face.

"The handle . . . right in front of you . . . pull on it."

Jaguar looked down, saw the handle and gave it a tug, then stood back and watched, in amazement, as the door swung open and lifted. They both got in, closed their doors, and Ignacio started the vehicle. The exhibition of lights on the dashboard mesmerized Jaguar.

This was a reaction Ignacio had grown accustomed to and had taken for granted by now.

Ignacio stomped on the clutch, shifted gears, and tore down the long alleyway. The sudden jerking of the vehicle made Jaguar grab his seat, looking for something to hold on to. As they reached the end of the alley, they exploded out onto the street as Ignacio hooked the car forcefully to the right, doing a slight fishtail.

Ignacio wanted to get some distance between the nightclub and himself just in case there was any chance his uncle may have been lurking around. As Ignacio's car sped down the road at top speeds, he finally slowed down to accommodate the speed limit in the area.

"So, where are we going? Where is this truck?" Jaguar asked.

"It's not too far from here. Maybe a couple of miles away."

What Jaguar could not have possibly known was the location Ignacio spoke of was the desert and the common graves' area. They headed out of the city, and were soon on an open highway, with the surrounding desert.

"So, this is how it goes down, huh? In the middle of the desert where no one can see you?" Jaguar asked.

"Something like that," Ignacio replied quietly.

He had taken an exit off the main highway, making a seamless transition into the desert. His headlights illuminated the ground in front of him. They helped him see through all the dirt and dust that the car was kicking up. Ignacio could hear gravel hitting the underbody of his very expensive vehicle, but it didn't matter to him.

He could buy a hundred more cars just like this one. Finally, as they approached what seemed to be an enormous mountain, Jaguar leaned forward to look up through the windshield, trying to find the top.

"Holy shit, we going up there?" he asked in awe.

"Yup . . . well, about halfway," Ignacio replied.

He drove up to a spot that had a trail that ran up alongside the mountain. He stopped the vehicle, positioning it so the headlights would light up the beginning of the path.

"Get out," Ignacio said.

By now, Ignacio's' entire demeanor had shifted, Jaguar not wise enough to pick up on it. Ignacio had flipped that switch in his mind, allowing his murder mentality to take over. He had Jaguar isolated, alone, and all to himself in the desert. Soon Jaguar would find out exactly how Ignacio had earned the name El Diablo.

Jaguar got out and looked at the full moon casting a luminescent light on the hills. He observed for a moment how alone and isolated it felt to be out here, but ignorantly thought nothing of it.

"Come on, let's go. They're waiting."

Ignacio had positioned himself at the start of the path. Jaguar joined him, and Ignacio motioned for him to take the lead. The path was nothing more than a narrow dirt trail with the mountain on one side and a steep drop on the other.

"How d'you get the trucks all the way up here?"

Jaguar asked.

"It's not the trucks, it's the other drivers we're meeting,"

Ignacio replied.

"But I don't see any other cars or vehicles out this way. It's just us," Jaguar shot back. His buzz was wearing off.

Jaguar began asking a lot of questions. It didn't matter to Ignacio, though. He had the van driver alone, in the desert, right where he wanted him.

"I told you I was behind. They all got here before us. They were dropped off a while ago, and they're waiting for us."

Ignacio paused.

"Let me ask you, how did you get the name Jaguar?"

Jaguar smiled.

"My homies gave it to me because I can run and fight. The police never catch me, and I've never lost a fight."

Ignacio chuckled.

"That's good. That's good."

What a fucking stupid way to get a nickname? He thought to himself. After they'd been walking for a while, they reached a small opening in the mountain. By now, they were high enough that the moon provided enough light to help guide their walk.

As they reached their landing, the moon's light revealed hundreds of shallow holes previously dug up from the ground. Ignacio, contemplating how he would make this kid disappear, lost his train of thought when Jaguar's phone suddenly rang.

"Oh shit, let me get that," Jaguar remarked.

Ignacio nodded, signaling to him that he should answer it. Jaguar fumbled for a moment, attempting to retrieve his phone from his pocket. Finally retrieving it, he answered.

"Hello? Yeah, hey, baby. I'm okay. We're here . . ."

Suddenly Ignacio put his finger up to his lips, signaling to Jaguar not to tell whoever he was speaking to where they were. Jaguar continued.

"I'm just out here with El Diablo, handling some shit. I'll be back later."

Ignacio turned, taking a few steps away from Jaguar, then turned back to face him. Ignacio appeared perfectly calm, without a trace of hesitation or apprehension in his body. He had been in this position before—it would be just another body in a long line of corpses.

It was merely the collateral damage that occurred from doing business with the De Los Santos family. As Jaguar hung up and tucked his phone back in his pocket, Ignacio grabbed his cell phone and pretended to receive a call.

With his thumb, Ignacio made sure that the volume was off, so in case the phone rang, Jaguar wouldn't hear it. Ignacio began speaking to dead air on the phone, giving a masterful performance of a fake conversation. Jaguar looked on intently, growing more and more inquisitive about who Ignacio could be speaking to.

"No. Yes. Yes, I get it . . . I get it. Yes, he's right here, do you wish to speak with him?"

Ignacio said.

Jaguar raised a brow. He grew inquisitive. Ignacio walked over to Jaguar, reached out his arm, and handed him the telephone.

"Here, my father wishes to speak with you."

Jaguar couldn't believe his ears, standing there in a state of disbelief. The head of the De Los Santos family wanted to speak with him personally? This would be such an honor. Jaguar stood there looking at Ignacio, who was staring back at him with a contrived smile on his face.

He gestured once again for Jaguar to take the phone.

"My father wishes to speak with you. He wants to speak with all the people who will be involved. This is a lot of weight we're moving. He needs to hear your voice."

With that last reassurance, Jaguar put the phone up to his ear.

"Hello?"

Within seconds Ignacio walked around Jaguar, now standing directly behind him. Quickly he grabbed Jaguar around the throat, placing him in a rear-naked choke, lifting him off the ground. Jaguar's short legs started flailing in the air. Jaguar attempted to reach behind his head, scratching and punching at Ignacio.

Jaguar managed to inflict tiny scratches on his face and eyes, but Ignacio was too strong. Ignacio said nothing, while he stood there with his arms tight around Jaguar's neck, listening to him grunt, gurgle, and gasp for air.

Eventually, all of Jaguar's thrashing became an annoyance to Ignacio.

He fell back to the ground, wrapping his legs tightly around Jaguar's body. Now he had him completely immobilized. After a few seconds, Jaguar was unconscious and at the complete and unholy mercy of El Diablo. When Ignacio was satisfied that Jaguar was unconscious, he loosened his grip around his neck, his body went completely limp.

Ignacio pushed the temporarily lifeless body of Jaguar off of him, rolling his body over face down. Ignacio stood up and brushed himself off. He reached down to pick up his phone, also grabbing Jaguar's phone out of his pocket. Ignacio removed his belt, then leaned over Jaguar's motionless body, grabbing both of his arms and hands, securing them behind his back with the belt.

Ignacio then turned Jaguar over on his back, unbuckled his pants, pulling them down around his ankles. This was an old trick Ignacio had learned many years ago. You can't run with your pants down around your ankles. Simple and effective.

Now that he had Jaguar completely compromised, he grabbed him by his shoulders lifting him up and slowly dragged him over to one of the shallow graves, which was only three or four feet deep. With a massive push, he tossed Jaguar's body in.

The fall jarred Jaguar back to consciousness, and immediately he started coughing and gasping for air. As Ruben lay face down in the grave, he rolled himself over to his side to see Ignacio standing at the foot of the hole. Still coughing, Jaguar attempted to speak.

"Come on, man. What the fuck? What are you doing? I thought I did a good job for you! I thought you needed another driver!"

"Another driver?"

Ignacio paused as he walked around the oblong-shaped grave.

"Another driver, no . . . no . . . I just needed to get you out of the nightclub to tie up some loose ends."

Ignacio now standing at the head of the grave. He bent down and peering at Jaguar.

"I have to say thank you, though. You made this way too easy for me. If you weren't so fucking stupid, then you would have known . . . you should have known that the instant I showed up at your table, out of the blue and unannounced, you were a dead man."

Ignacio chuckled.

"I mean, why would I honestly need a piss ant such as yourself to drive a load for me, huh?"

Ignacio spat on Jaguar, then stood up and walked away.

"Stupid pendejo." He muttered under his breath.

Ignacio walked a few feet away from the shallow grave and pulled out his gun from the back of his pants. He paused, looking at it, admiring it. Ignacio walked back to the foot of the grave, aiming the gun down at Jaguar, who had forced his way up to a kneeling position.

He stared up at Ignacio, saying nothing. Ignacio broke the silence between them.

"You have a big mouth, Jaguar. I find it hard to believe you said nothing to no one, so I want to know who you told about the driving job Diego gave you."

Jaguar stared at Ignacio, saying nothing. Ignacio irritated, raised his voice,

"Maybe you hit your head, and you don't hear too well, so I will ask you again. Who did you tell about the job?"

He cocked the hammer on the gun and extended his arm.

"Go ahead and do what you're going to do, fool. I ain't scared of you," Jaguar replied, with a defiant tone in his voice.

"I've had guns pointed at me my entire life, you ain't showing me anything."

Ignacio stood there for a few seconds contemplating what to do, suddenly BANG! He shot Jaguar in his right leg as he kneeled in the grave. Jaguar let out a blood-curdling scream and keeled over. Then, just as quickly, two more gunshots rang out into the night air, sending echoes throughout the moonlit valley. Ignacio had shot Jaguar in his left leg and shoulder.

The gunshot to his shoulder thrust Jaguar down on his back. His cries grew loud. Ignacio let him lie there writhing in pain.

"Okay, asshole. Let's try this again. One last time, who did you tell about driving that van for me?"

"I didn't tell anyone, okay? I didn't say anything to anyone!" Jaguar screamed back at him. By this time, Jaguar rolled on the ground in excruciating pain.

"Bullshit! A kid like you, big ego and a big mouth, and you didn't say anything to anyone? I find that hard to believe."

"It's the truth; man, c'mon . . . Mr. De Los Santos, please!" Jaguar started to plead for his life.

"What did you do with the van after the job was done?"

"We drove it back to the place where we got it from. The chop shop."

Ignacio could feel his stomach drop.

"So, you picked it up from the shop and returned it to the same place?"

"Yes, that's what I was told to do."

By now, Jaguar's breathing was heavy.

Ignacio knew precisely who had told him to do such a stupid thing. Now, the one piece of evidence that could link him to his father's attempted murder was sitting at his very own business. What the hell was Diego thinking?

Ignacio realized that time had run its course, and Jaguar would have told him just about anything if he thought he would get out of this. Ignacio had set out to do what he wanted, eliminate the bomb maker and the van driver. The two closest pieces linking him to the attack on his father.

Ignacio looked down at his watch. Now nearly 3 o'clock in the morning, he needed to think about getting back to the compound to his mother and father. Plus, he needed to think about getting his hands on that damn van and what story he would tell his mother about why he was gone all day.

La Familia: Loose Ends

And, of course, whether he had found any clues as to who perpetrated the attack. Ignacio shoved his gun back into the back of his pants. He glared down at Jaguar, who by now had been reduced to whimpering shell of a man. Ignacio noticed a small shovel about fifty feet away, walking over to retrieve it, he snatched it out of a small mound of dirt next to a freshly dug grave awaiting an occupant.

The Common Graves was a remote area used primarily for those who weren't claimed by anyone. Their bodies sitting in the morgue at the coroner's office. The Common Graves provided the lost and nameless souls some sort of a decent burial. For Ignacio's purposes, it was the perfect place for someone like Jaguar to disappear, and no one would be the wiser.

With the small shovel in his hand, Ignacio walked back to Jaguar's shallow grave, and began shoveling dirt into the hole. Jaguar's whimpers now became soft cries as he realized he was going to be buried alive, and this was how his life would end. Scoop by scoop, Ignacio tossed piles of dirt and rocks into the small crater.

Too weak and in too much pain to do anything else, Jaguar laid there as inevitably his feet, his legs, then torso were covered. Lastly, Ignacio buried his head. It had taken Ignacio just twenty minutes to eliminate Jaguar and return him back to the earth, burying him alive. He stamped down the ground with his feet to make sure the dirt was packed tight, and to ensure there would be no chance of this loose end crawling his way out.

Once done, he walked the shovel back over to its original location, threw it back into the small mound of dirt, and started his journey back down the narrow trail. As he reached the bottom of the mountain, he couldn't help but wonder how he was going to spin this entire thing.

What was he going to tell his mother about what he had discovered? Had his father awakened yet? Was he asking questions? How far along was his uncle in his investigation? And now the van had to be eliminated too.

Ignacio knew he needed to devise a rock-solid plan with an impenetrable story to frame someone. Unfortunately, he also knew his scheme would come at a tremendous personal cost. Still, he was willing to make that sacrifice to be king someday. He climbed into his vehicle, started the engine, and sped off into the night headed back to the De Los Santos compound.

Chapter 6: The Investigation

Aurelio had locked down the entire De Los Santos home, now neck deep into his investigation. He had all the local and state police at his disposal and appeared to be using every man available to him. Nighttime had fallen, the rain had come and gone providing some relief from the heat, but it now made his crime scene harder to process.

Large white tents had been constructed throughout the property. They helped shield the remaining evidence from being lost or contaminated. Enormous construction lights lit up the entire property, leaving not one square inch in the dark.

Wearing raincoats, bomb technicians, crime scene analysts, and medical examiners scoured endlessly, all hard at work combing throughout the area. The news media had set up a small camp of their own right outside the secured gates to the property. A dozen news reporters all clamored to get the first word out on the breaking news of the investigation.

By now, most of the dead had been removed and taken to the coroner's office to await further examination and identification. However, the smell of death still loomed in the dense air. Bomb-sniffing dogs and their handlers remained hard at work, tracking every piece of explosive material they could find around the pool area.

A shorter man approached Aurelio with a clipboard.

"Lieutenant, we finally have an official count, sir."

Aurelio took a big breath in and exhaled.

"Very well, let me hear it."

"Fifteen total dead, sir. Eight children and seven adults. Four men, three women. Four children are still at the hospital. They're being kept for observation overnight. Five men have been treated and released, and two women refused to be seen, and of course, none of them are willing to talk to us."

Aurelio stood with his head down, staring at the ground.

"Jesus Christ," he muttered as he turned and walked away.

He tore open a Velcro pocket on his bullet-proof vest, pulling out his cell phone. He pressed two buttons to autodial a number for him.

After four rings, a man's voice answered on the other end.

"Hello?"

Aurelio looked up to the sky with apprehension in his heart. His words momentarily stuck in his throat.

"Mayor Vargas, its Lieutenant De Los Santos, sir. There is an update for you. It's not good."

"How bad is it?"

"Eight dead children, sir, and seven adults."

"What the hell?" the mayor snapped. "Were any of the dead your family?"

"No, sir."

"I would start there. Obviously, this is a high-profile case, Lieutenant. You have always been an outstanding police officer, and I've never had to question your judgment or loyalty. The rule of law has always dominated your decision-making. That's one of the few reasons I'm allowing you to work on this case. You'll be able to get closer than anyone else. But you better play this one by the book. Am I clear? The letter of the law."

"Yes, sir, I will. I am all over it. I'm aware of the stakes, sir." Aurelio replied.

"I will expect a report first thing in the morning."

Without saying goodbye, the mayor ended the call.

Aurelio was not a drinker, but at this point, a few shots of tequila sounded great to him. Still staring at his phone, he smashed his fingers into two buttons to autodial another number. The phone rang several times before someone finally picked up.

"Yes?" a woman's voice answered.

"Gabriella, it's me, Aurelio. How is everyone?"

His tone remained calm. Despite his loyalty to his job, he cared deeply for his family, even though the feeling was not always reciprocated.

"Vicente is fine. He's resting. Lucita is okay. She's sleeping right now."

"And you? How are you?" Aurelio asked.

Gabriella cracked a subtle smile.

"I am fine, Aurelio." she paused a moment.

"How is my house?" she asked.

"Well, it's crawling with local and state police at the moment.

Am I going to find anything I shouldn't?"

"Of course not, don't be ridiculous." Gabriella responded, sounding slightly offended.

Aurelio cracked a smile.

"I'm standing here in the rain waiting on your guest list. You promised you'd have it to me by the end of the day. I assume that someone is coming?"

"Yes, I am sending one of my men over right now with the list."

Gabriella knowing full well that what she just told him was a complete lie. She sat right next to Vicente still monitoring him. She had directed no one to do anything yet, realizing she would now she need to send Diego over with a list.

"Good, tell your man he won't be able to access the house. When he reaches the front gate, he'll need to inform my men to radio me; I'll come out and get it from him."

"Very well," Gabriella replied and hung up the phone.

#

Gabriella spun around in her chair and walked to the metal doors. When she reached the hallway, she saw one of the guards standing at the door leading to the outside.

"Go upstairs and tell Diego I need him immediately."

Without waiting for the guard to acknowledge her, she turned and walked back into the room.

The guard walked down the long hallway, using the quick bursts of lightening to help illuminate his path. Each strike touched the small stained-glass windows, spattering incredible shades of orange, green, and purple hues onto the brick wall. The guard reached the long metal staircase and made his way up.

When he reached the top, he opened the large red door, and observed Diego standing, staring at the floor, pinching the bridge of his nose with his fingers. He held his phone in his other hand tightly. Hearing the door open, he lifted his head and turned to the guard and asked,

"What do you want?"

"Señora De Los Santos has requested your presence downstairs right away."

"Very well, I will be down in a second. Close the door," he replied.

The guard turned around and closed the door behind him. Diego stood there leaning against a counter, reflecting on his conversation with Ignacio. He understood that now he was in danger of being considered a loose end. Before he left the room to speak with Gabriella, he checked in on Lucita one last time.

She lay curled up resting comfortably on the couch clutching her teddy bear. Diego turned and headed toward the door, closing it softly behind him. Diego made his way down the staircase and through the long hallway. As he approached the doors to the infirmary, he peeked inside and witnessed Gabriella sitting by Vicente's side. Pushing his way in slowly, he stopped slightly after he got past the door. He cleared his throat.

"Señora De Los Santos, you wanted to speak to me?"

Gabriella spun around in her chair.

"Yes, I did. I need you to take this list over to the house and drop it off with Aurelio."

Diego looked confused.

"Señora?"

"I promised Aurelio a list of our guests. Of course, I'm not going to give him the actual one, but we need to steer him in the direction we want and control his investigation. At least until Ignacio gets back and fills me in on what he has found. Speaking of which, where the hell is he, where is my son?"

Diego realizing he could not answer Gabriella truthfully, had to tell her something. Otherwise, she would start to grow suspicious.

"I just got off the phone with him a little while ago. He said he is on his way back, but did not want to say what he found; over the phone, only that he had something."

Gabriella looked down at her watch, seeing it now was closing in on 4 o'clock in the morning.

"Good, I will be curious to see what he has to say."

She walked over to the desk and pulled open the top drawer. Inside she found an old yellow writing pad and a pencil. She pulled them out, bent down over the desk, and started writing. Diego waited while she scribbled down names.

"When you reach the front gate," she said, while continuing to write her list, "you will need to tell Aurelio's men to radio up to him. He will come down and get this list from you. If he starts to ask you any questions, you are only permitted to tell him we are fine, and that everyone is doing okay, is that clear?"

"Yes, Señora, and if he asks me anything about the party?"

Gabriella stopped writing and looked up at him.

"What do you mean? Are you listening? You are to say nothing. Play dumb. You have no idea what happened. If you start answering my brother-in-law's questions, he will use anything you give him as ammunition against us and will twist your words around. Is that something you are willing to take a chance on?"

"No, Señora, absolutely not."

Diego's tone sounding humble.

"Very well, then. You will only tell him we are okay."

She looked back down at her piece of paper and added three more names. Folding the piece of paper in half, she handed it to him.

"Now go and hurry right back."

Diego nodded, turned around, and left the room, pushing his way through the metal doors. As he made his way down the hallway to the front door, he unfolded the piece of paper to take a glance. Gabriella had written ten names on the list, none of which he recognized, except one, a child's name. Alejandra Rivera.

Diego recognized her instantly; she was Lucita's best friend and the daughter of a very powerful and dangerous man. Diego served as the girls' bodyguard when he escorted them out of the compound. He liked her. She smiled all the time, used her manners and was polite. She always said thank you. Diego struggled with his thoughts, wondering if she had been killed as a result of his actions.

As he pushed his way through the large wooden door and out into the parking area, the sky finally seemed to clear. The clouds separated; the night appeared quiet. Before he climbed in his vehicle, Diego stopped and gazed up into the sky and admired the fantastic moon.

He wondered what the next few days would hold for him and what his subsequent conversation with Ignacio would look like. A part of him still held out hope that his lifelong friendship with

Ignacio would get him through this mess. They had grown up together, slept in the same bed as kids, and ran from the police together.

He kept some of Ignacio's deepest secrets, including this one. There wasn't anything he wouldn't do for his best friend, even if he had earned the nickname El Diablo. With that final thought, he climbed into his vehicle and raced back to the De Los Santos home.

#

After he hung up the phone with Gabriella, Aurelio gathered all of his lead detectives for a status update. As he started walking in the direction of the pool area, Aurelio let out a high-pitched whistle, everyone stopped and looked up from what they were doing.

"Update meeting. My vehicle. Five minutes!" he yelled.

Then turning back around to walk to his car. Everyone else returned to scouring the crime scene for evidence. Aurelio sat on the hood of his police car with his foot on the bumper, waiting patiently for his people to arrive. This was a tough situation for him to wrap his mind around.

Not only because of the dead children, also because of the attack against his family. As he sat there, one-by-one, the lead investigators made their way over to the vehicle. They stood in front of Aurelio in a half-circle formation. Some investigators carried clipboards with scribbled notes.

When everyone arrived at the car, Aurelio recognized the exhaustion in their faces.

"Thank you all for your hard work. I realize this has been an extremely long day for you. I need an update on what we have at this point so I can start putting together my report for the Mayor."

A woman wearing a white rain poncho raised her hand and jumped right in without hesitation.

"I'll start."

Aurelio nodded his head and pointed at her to acknowledge her.

"Good. Go."

"It looks like they wrapped the bomb in one of the presents. Definitely mixed in with all the others. It had a certain level of sophistication to it."

"What do you mean a certain level of sophistication?"

Aurelio asked.

"I found small pieces of a mercury switch. You don't find that in bombs every day. And whoever made this used nitroglycerin along with . . ."

"Nitroglycerin?"

Aurelio interrupted.

"Yes, sir."

Aurelio rubbed his face. He could only think of one person who made bombs with such devastating force. He had arrested a guy over a decade ago, for a bombing that killed several people at a park, but he kept this thought to himself for the time being.

"Go on, continue."

"From what I gather, the mercury switch was supposed to be used as the trigger, but I don't think it ever had a chance to work. Something that you need to understand when you use nitroglycerin, anything can set it off—a minor bump, or excessive heat, then BOOM!"

Aurelio began thinking out loud. "But why would you not use a timer in this situation? The thing was capable of exploding in transport, or the second it got here. A timer made more sense in an unpredictable setting."

The young technician continued,

"We'll continue working to piece the bomb back together, sir. That's about all I can tell you."

"All right, thank you. You can go back and continue."

As the investigator stepped away, Aurelio looked over at his lead medical examiner.

"You're up next. What do you have?"

"It's ugly, but that's no surprise. We've got bodies and pieces of bodies, everywhere. I have to say, though, I am surprised there aren't more dead, considering how close in proximity all the guests were when the bomb detonated. We've tagged all the bodies, and they are being transported to my office. My team is starting the identification process while I am here. I will inform you when we've finished."

"Good, thank you. I appreciate it."

Aurelio paused, glancing at the man standing next to him,

"Okay, who's next?"

Sergeant Ramos spoke up.

"As it stands right now, there is no obvious motive for the attack. It looks like all the dead are civilians, no one connected directly to the cartels. We'll have more knowledge once the bodies are identified. I'm only speculating, but I believe the intended target was someone in your family."

Aurelio stood up from the hood of his car to face and stand closer to his friend.

"Yeah, I'm starting to think the same thing. But the crazy thing is this; no one from my family is dead. My brother's condition is serious, but he's still alive."

Aurelio paused diving deep into his thoughts staring at the ground for a moment, eventually dismissing the group, realizing he had absolutely no solid leads, feeling no closer to solving this attack than he had hours ago. As he stood there at his police cruiser trying to sift through his thoughts, he realized a young man standing behind him at the trunk of his car.

He wasn't wearing a rain jacket like everyone else. However, his police credentials hanging around his neck identified him as a cyber technician. He was holding an open laptop. Aurelio walked over to him.

"What do you have there?"

"I think you need to see this, sir."

The young man paused, spinning the laptop around so the screen faced Aurelio. A video was paused, showing the front entrance of the De Los Santos home earlier in the day before the attack. The time stamp on the video read 2 o'clock in the afternoon.

"I accessed the video surveillance footage of the home, looking for any evidence and, well . . . I'll just let you watch."

The technician tapped the play button on the laptop, Aurelio viewed guests arriving at the home. Gabriella stood at the front entrance wearing her white outfit, greeting guests. Small children climbed out of limousines, running into her arms as she bent down to give them hugs.

After five minutes had elapsed in the video, Aurelio witnessed a large white van pull up a short distance to the front of the house and stop. A small, short guy climbed out of the driver's side seat. About ten seconds later, Diego came into view and greeted the van driver.

They shook hands as Diego pointed in the general direction of the pool area, eventually disappearing from view as the driver walked to the back of the van.

Aurelio's stare grew intense as he tried to process what he was seeing. The short young tattooed driver walked to the rear of the van, opening both doors, pulling out a medium-size gift-wrapped box. Aurelio's heart rate increased. His arms tensed as he crossed them in front of his body.

Every ligament and tendon flexed. He stared at the man that looked extremely out of place carrying the package, studying everything about him. The driver walked the package in the direction of the pool, out of the range of the security camera. Aurelio's head shot up, looking at the young technician.

"Please tell me you have footage of the pool area?"

Aurelio asked.

The young man nodded, pressing a few buttons on the laptop. The screen cut to security camera footage of the patio where the party was taking place. This time Aurelio had a better understanding of the layout and where everyone had been positioned. Seconds later, the driver of the van came walking into view carrying the package.

His demeanor seemed relaxed, not necessarily what you'd expect of someone carrying an explosive device. Aurelio wondered if the guy had any idea what he was even carrying. The driver walked directly over to a table, placing the gift with the other presents, positioned next to the location where Vicente sat.

After setting the package down, the driver paused briefly to soak in all the surrounding activity, then turned and walked back the way he came.

"Get me back to that first camera in front of the house,"

Aurelio snapped.

The technician quickly tapped two buttons on the keypad, switching to the view from the first security camera. Aurelio continued to scrutinize the driver as he came back into sight and walked toward the van. Before reaching the van, Diego appeared in the frame once again walking out of the family home. This time Diego approached him, handing him what appeared to be a small white envelope. The driver opened the envelope, smiled, and placed it in his back pocket before eventually climbing in the van. As he drove away, Diego walked back toward the house.

"Pause it!"

Aurelio hollered as he reached into a pocket on his vest, pulling out a small notepad and pen. He then leaned in toward the screen to get the license plate of the van.

"GFH . . . 29 . . . 87. I got you, asshole!"

He muttered, closing his notepad and tucking the pen back into his vest pocket. He nodded to the technician.

"Okay, continue."

The young man tapped the start button, and Aurelio witnessed the white van take off down the driveway. It didn't leave with any sense of urgency, so Aurelio wondered again if the guy realized what was in the package. Regardless, he was a major suspect and as responsible for everyone's death as whoever ordered the hit.

"Take me back to the pool, if you will,"

Aurelio asked.

He briefly closed his eyes taking in a big deep breath knowing he was about to see the murder of all those children. The young technician clicked a couple of buttons; Aurelio began watching the camera footage of the pool and gazebo area. Kids were playing, running around laughing, and having a great time.

Adults could be seen sitting at tables talking, holding casual conversations. The band was playing. Vicente's had his men stationed all around the inner perimeter, holding their weapons as they walked around. They were oblivious to what was about to befall them.

Aurelio's curiosity started to tingle as he eyeballed Vicente sitting at the head table talking with three older men, all of whom he recognized.

"I'll be damned. Holy shit!" he whispered to himself.

The long-held tradition among Mexican drug lords and cartels was independence. There had never been a hierarchy established.

La Familia: Loose Ends

Everyone operated independently and in competition with each other, but Vicente De Los Santos was a distinct type of animal.

He had established the Junta Directiva, a "Board of Directors." Placing each man in charge of a sector of Mexico. From Juarez, Tijuana, Sinaloa, Guadalajara, and Mexico City, each man had responsibility for his region and plaza.

All the men Vicente sat with were heads of their respective cartels, composed of Felix Rivera, Cesar Reyes, and Guillermo Salazar. Still, Vicente was the boss of bosses, better known as "El Jefe." Aurelio desperately wanted to hear their conversation.

What extraordinary Intel could be gathered to topple their mighty empires however, the video didn't record audio, so he was left to wonder. Vicente stood up, grabbing a glass of champagne, then walked around the table to a microphone stand. He tapped the side of his glass with a fork.

Guests stopped what they were doing, the band stopped playing, and everyone turned to give Vicente their complete attention. Aurelio assumed he was giving a speech in recognition of his daughter's birthday. Vicente turned to face the house soon Gabriella came walking into the picture.

She had a champagne glass in her hand and joined Vicente at the microphone. He wrapped his arm around her waist as they looked happy and were smiling. Vicente spoke for a brief moment afterwards as he raised his glass.

All the guests toasted acknowledging his speech and proceeded to drink, Gabriella gave Vicente a kiss soon after stepping out of frame. Vicente turned and made his way back to the table where he had been sitting previously. A quick flash of light consumed the screen not too long after the camera went black.

Aurelio looked up at the young technician and snatched the laptop out of his hands, spinning around to place it on the back of his car.

"Show me how to work this thing."

The technician quickly showed him four essential functions, stop, start, pause, and switching camera angles.

"Okay . . . sorry to be rude, kid, but beat it,"

Aurelio barked at him.

He wanted to take his time and playback the video as many times as he needed to, dissecting the series of events he had just discovered. Over and over again, forward, rewind, forward, rewind, Aurelio studied the video, trying to glean any bit of information he could. He started the video at the point where Vicente turned to walk back to his table.

The timestamp read two thirty-five, so approximately thirty-five minutes after the bomb was placed on the gift table. Aurelio paused the video at the exact second the explosion occurred. Two things stood out to him. First, he made note on how close the bomb was to Vicente and the Junta Directiva.

It was maybe twenty feet away, so this definitely may have been an assassination attempt on the entire group. In addition, seconds before the explosion, Vicente passed by a giant concrete statue of a lion—probably what had shielded him from the full force of the blast saving his life.

Aurelio stood straight up and looked out at the pool area, once again taking in a big breath. He let out a huge exhale of air, now even more frustrated.

Presented now with a hundred more questions than answers, and his mind was racing a thousand miles an hour. Who would benefit from killing the entire Board of Directors? Were they even the target? Why kill innocent children in the process, especially his beautiful niece?

La Familia: Loose Ends

Who was that van driver, and where was that van? Ultimately, one person dominated his thoughts and ran through his mind the most, Diego. He didn't like the guy at all. He was a slick talker, arrogant, acted very much like Ignacio with a sense of entitlement.

This was a significant break for Aurelio, he witnessed Diego on video greeting the van driver and handing something to him. He needed to get his hands-on Diego. He closed the laptop, picked it up, and turned around and started walking toward one of the large crime scene tents on the property.

His walk was slow, as fatigue started to set in. When Aurelio reached the tent, he saw the young cyber technician sitting in a chair working on another computer. He walked over to the young man and held out the laptop.

"Make sure you make several copies of these files."

The technician turned around in his chair and looked up at Aurelio.

"Yes, sir, I already have. Everything's been backed up."

"Good, thank you."

Aurelio placed the laptop on the table and walked away.

Just then, a man's voice called out to Aurelio over his radio.

"Lieutenant, there is someone at the front gate to see you."

Aurelio reached up; grabbing the small radio strapped to his shoulder,

"Who is it?"

"He says he's one of the De Los Santos men, sir, Diego."

Aurelio became excited.

"Keep him there, I'll be right down,"

Aurelio shot back. Of all the men Gabriella could have sent to him, what dumb luck? Perhaps he should buy a lottery ticket. Even though Aurelio was eager to speak with Diego, he did not hurry to get down to him; he knew his men would keep him there.

Before he left the tent, Aurelio poured himself a cup of coffee. He needed something to help keep his energy up. Aurelio did not have many vices. He wasn't a drinker. He ate well and exercised regularly, but coffee was his one weakness. On his way down to the front gate, he took small slow sips of his coffee, savoring each one.

He also enjoyed the rush of having a key suspect in his hands. Something he loved. Aurelio strolled down a tiny hill which eventually led to the large metal gates. A rather large, beautiful concrete wall that ran around the perimeter of the property surrounded the entire yard.

He strolled his way past two police vehicles that blocked access to the primary entrance of the house. As he approached, he could see that it was a media circus outside. Barriers and partitions had been set up to keep the news and television reporters at bay. They all stirred when they noticed Aurelio walking down the hill.

Television cameramen turned on their bright lamps, illuminating the front yard. As he reached the gate, Aurelio could see Diego's car surrounded on both sides with reporters. He signaled to his men at the gate to open it. After Diego drove through, the gates remained open.

Reporters pushed into each other, yelling out questions, thrusting their microphones in his direction as cameras flashed. It was loud and chaotic; Aurelio couldn't make out what any of them were saying. He walked up to Diego's car, tapped his finger on the driver's side window, and signaled for him not to move.

Aurelio then walked over to the gate where the reporters were standing and raised both of his arms, finally signaling for them to calm down, the crowd quickly fell silent.

He paused for a moment.

"I will make a very brief statement but will not be answering questions."

Aurelio sucked in a big breath of air.

La Familia: Loose Ends

"Earlier today, there was an attack on the De Los Santos property. Fifteen people are confirmed dead, including eight children and seven adults. We are working on confirming their identities and notifying their families. This case is still under investigation, and I do not have any further comment for you at this time."

As Aurelio turned and walked away, the swarm of media erupted again, yelling out questions. He walked back to Diego's vehicle and tapped on the window once again. The window rolled down, and Aurelio saw Diego in the driver's seat.

"Pull in and park to the side." Diego nodded.

Aurelio started to smile. He savored the taste of the fly landing in the spider's web. He approached Diego's car as he was getting out. Aurelio locked eyes with him.

"Well, well, well, look what the cat dragged in,"

Aurelio said.

"Of all the men Gabriella could have sent over, she sent her errand boy."

He was trying to spark a reaction in Diego, but Diego remained calm and said nothing. He reached in his front pocket and retrieved the list Gabriella had given him, handing it to Aurelio.

"Here, you're supposed to have this," he said in a bland, dismissive tone, not wanting to engage Aurelio in conversation. As Aurelio grabbed the note, Diego turned around and climbed back in his vehicle. In his mind, he had done his job and was going back to the compound.

"Hey . . . whoa . . . slow down there cowboy, where you going so fast?"

Diego swung back around and looked at Aurelio, standing there with a cocky look on his face.

"What do you mean? You have the guest list, and it's time for me to go." Diego said.

"Yeah, but I have some questions for you first."

Aurelio smiled.

"How is everyone?"

That was a question Diego understood he could answer.

"Everyone is fine. Lucita, Gabriella, Vicente, they are all good."

His response was stiff and cold.

"And Ignacio . . . how is he?"

Diego's heart began to beat just a little faster, but he kept his cool.

"Ignacio is good. He's with his parents right now."

"That's good. That's really good."

Aurelio's tone was smooth, almost condescending. He paused, looking down at the paper Diego had handed him. He unfolded it and read the list of names.

"Hmm, only ten people were at the party? It seemed like a lot more to me on the security footage I watched."

Aurelio looked back up at Diego, waiting for his response.

Diego's stomach dropped. He felt instantly sick. *Shit, the security cameras!* If Aurelio had watched the security footage, then he must have seen him meeting the van driver. He continued to give Aurelio a blank look, hoping the panic wasn't showing on his face.

"If Señora De Los Santos said it was ten, then it was ten."

Diego did not like this cat-and-mouse game that was being played.

"Where were you when the bomb exploded?"

Aurelio asked.

Diego now feeling himself getting sucked in to Aurelio's vortex realized this was a question he definitely could not answer, but what should he do? Gabriella said Aurelio was a master at using his words against him. And just like that, in a few quick seconds, Aurelio had engulfed him into a line of questioning.

He was screwed.

"Hey, look, I have to get back to the compound. Señora De Los Santos is waiting for me."

Diego tried to explain while pretending to stay calm.

Aurelio, sensing the shift in Diego's demeanor, and began to bait him harder.

"Oh yeah, right. Gabriella is waiting. Would you like me to call her and tell her you are okay? Tell her you are here with me?"

Aurelio reached into his front pocket, pulling out his cell phone and started waving it in Diego's face.

"NO!"

Diego just about jumped out of his skin, slightly lunging forward, holding out his hand to stop him.

"No, there is no need to do that." The inflection in his voice said he was rattled.

"You sure? I can just call her for you."

Diego leaned against the side of his vehicle, placing his arm on the roof and his hand on his head.

"No man, I'm good. You don't have to call her."

Aurelio smiled and placed the phone back in his pocket.

"Why don't you go ahead and turn the engine off."

Diego nervously shifted from one foot to the other, reaching inside to turn off the ignition.

"So, you never answered me, where were you when the bomb went off?"

Aurelio pressed him again.

At this point, Diego knew he was trapped and had nowhere to go.

"I was inside, monitoring the house."

"You weren't concerned about guarding the family?"

Aurelio asked.

"No, there were plenty of men outside. My job was to cover the inside, make sure no one tried to go where they shouldn't."

Aurelio reached into his pants pocket and pulled out a stick of chewing gum. As he started unwrapping it, he casually leaned back against Diego's car.

"Did you speak to anyone at the party?"

"Like who?" Diego asked, shrugging his shoulders.

"I don't know . . . anyone."

Aurelio was trying to maintain a good poker face. He sensed it was only a matter of time before Diego would say something he shouldn't.

"Nope, I didn't talk to anyone."

"So, when did you greet the van driver? I mean, since you were inside patrolling the house and all."

Diego's heart stopped; he could feel his pupils dilate. He had a tightness in his chest, his legs grew weak. *FUCK!* He thought to himself. Good thing he was leaning against his car. Otherwise, he would have probably dropped to the ground. Diego remained silent.

"Well, I'm waiting. When did you greet the van driver? You remember that short little guy that was carrying the bomb?"

By now, Aurelio tipped his hand completely. He would not show this scumbag any mercy. He knew he had him right where he wanted him. Checkmate!

Diego just stood there motionless, saying nothing, realizing he just messed up. Still, there was no way Aurelio could completely tie him to Jaguar. He hadn't accused him of the attack; he merely asked him about the van driver.

Even though Diego assumed his life was over, he would attempt to play along and see if he could throw Aurelio off. However, he made no illusions, this was going to be a dangerous game to play.

"I was walking around the house as I said. I just entered the living room when I looked out the front window and saw a white van pull up. So, I walked out to see what was up. The guy driving the van said he had a delivery, a package for the party, and asked me where it was supposed to go. I told him all deliveries go around to the pool area. That was it."

"I've known you all your life, Diego. And I have no doubts you are a cold-blooded killer just like my nephew. I have never known you to shake someone's hand you just met. When the guy gets out, you greet him, that's not just showing someone where a package goes. Did you know there was a bomb inside?"

Diego postured his body stiff as a board.

"What? Of course not! How the hell would I have known that? Do you think I would have let that shit through? I would have dropped that pendejo right where he stood. How you gonna ask me some bullshit like that?"

Diego's attempt at defiance and outrage fell on deaf ears.

Aurelio took a few steps toward Diego. His size was intimidating for most people, but to Diego, he seemed like a giant. His muscular physique and deep voice were rattling him and he had him backed into a corner. Aurelio's tone was stern, his glare was hard,

"Because I know you, and I know my nephew. Do I think you have balls big enough to kill the entire Junta Directiva? Maybe, maybe not, but something in that damn video looks suspicious to me. What did you hand him after he dropped the package off and walked back to the van?"

Aurelio's eyes were now wide, his nostrils flared just a little, his mannerisms were intense. He was in full cop mode and wanted to make Diego sweat. Aurelio was leaning in closer to him. He was just mere inches away from his face. Finally irritated at his lack of quick response, Aurelio poked Diego in his chest bone.

"Hey asshole, my little niece was almost murdered today. Eight little children lost their lives. You think Vicente is a gangster? You haven't dealt with me yet!"

Diego had nowhere to go. He knew that Aurelio had him with the video, although he didn't have the smoking gun just yet. So, at best, he was bluffing. Otherwise, he would have already thrown him in handcuffs. It was still too early in his investigation to have any concrete proof of his involvement.

However, Diego knew that he was at a crossroads. As much anxiety as he felt, he was still a soldier for the De Los Santos family, and being a rat was not an option. Betraying Ignacio or Vicente De Los Santos only assured him of one thing: the fastest death, a bullet to the head.

"I watched the guy walk the package to the back and drop it off," Diego finally replied.

"When he came back, he said he hadn't been paid for the delivery. I handed him an envelope with some money, and then he left."

Aurelio stepped back a bit and softened his posture. He broke out in a slight chuckle as he scratched his face and then looked down.

"So, you mean to tell me you just happened to have a random amount of money on you in a white envelope, and you used it to pay some delivery guy who said he hadn't been paid yet?"

Aurelio took a few steps back and turned when he reached the trunk of Diego's car. He spun around to look out at the media, then turned back to face Diego.

"You know what? Don't even bother answering that."

Aurelio threw both arms in the air letting them slam back down to his side. He slowly walked toward Diego, pointing his finger at him.

"I'll tell you what, though. If you think you and I are done, you have another thing coming. I told you if you lied to me it was going to be a bad day for you, and well . . . now you're gonna feel every inch of me!"

Aurelio's cell phone rang, snatching it out of his vest pocket he looked at the incoming number and took the call.

"Hello, Lieutenant De Los Santos here."

He could hear sirens in the background.

"Lieutenant, this is Fire Commander Alvarez. You're not going to believe this one!" the caller said as Aurelio stood glaring at Diego.

"I'm over here on Calle Violetas and Calle Las Flores. There's been another massive explosion. We just extinguished the blaze."

Aurelio was intrigued. He motioned to Diego to stay put as he stepped away from him so he wouldn't overhear the call.

"Why are you calling me? I have my own investigation here."

"Well, you see Lieutenant, here's the thing. We found a body inside the building with a bullet hole to the back of the head. We also found a ton of explosive materials on the premises. I'm not talking about a few sticks of dynamite. I'm talking plastic explosives, undetonated dynamite, nitroglycerin, and . . ."

"Wait, stop. Say that again." Now the fire commander had Aurelio's complete and undivided attention.

"I said we found plastic explosives."

"Yeah, I heard you say all of that, what was that last one?"

"We found traces of nitroglycerin."

Aurelio, now, about twenty feet away from Diego, whipped around to lock eyes with him. Aurelio's inner suspicions were screaming at him there had to be a connection between the two explosions.

"Commander, I'm sending one of my men over there right now to oversee the investigation until I get there.

Make sure you give him full access to anything he needs. And until I get there, don't let anyone touch that body, do you understand?"

"Yes, Lieutenant, I understand."

Aurelio ended the call and made his way back to Diego. At this point, he was ready to tackle this matter head-on. Tired of Diego's bullshit he asked him flat out,

"Don't suppose you can tell me anything about an explosion over in the slums? They found a body."

Diego looked back at him with a confused look on his face, but inside he knew this had Ignacio written all over it. It had to be the bomb maker.

"Nope, sure don't. I've been with the family this entire time. They can vouch for me."

Diego's tone was a little cocky.

Aurelio put his phone back in his vest.

"You know, that sounds like a magnificent idea. Perhaps I should speak to the family. Let's head over to the compound. I'll follow you. Give me a minute to get my vehicle, and I'll meet you here at the gate."

Aurelio began to walk up the small hill back toward the house.

Diego's heart once again descended into the deepest part of his chest. He tried to comprehend how he had just been so easily outplayed. His hands shook. Diego twisted around watching Aurelio walk back up the hill and screamed,

"Wait, what, say that again . . . you want me to do what?"

Aurelio kept walking without looking back. He yelled over his shoulder.

"We're going to go and see the family." Then he stopped and swung around to look at Diego.

"Why is there a problem?"

Diego did not respond. He turned and got into his vehicle. He sat there, thinking about what he had just done. How was he going to explain this to Ignacio and Gabriella? He could feel Aurelio's claws digging into him. He had no idea how he would get himself out of this one.

La Familia: Loose Ends

A few minutes later, he started the ignition when he saw Aurelio's vehicle coming down the driveway. His headlights temporarily blinded Diego. Aurelio pulled up alongside him, rolling down his window. Diego did the same.

"I'll have to go first; my men will let us out. We'll drive past all the media, then you can get in front of me and lead the way."

With that, Aurelio rolled his window back up and drove toward the front gate. Diego pulled in behind him. The gates opened, and they both slowly pulled out. As they drove by the media, the flashing lights of the cameras and bright lights of the television news crews flooded their windows.

They drove to the end of the driveway, Aurelio pulled over, allowing Diego to pass. They then pulled out onto the main road and headed to the De Los Santos compound.

Chapter 7: Family Reunion

The sun slowly commenced to rise, signaling the start of another day. The room was quiet except for the beeping sound from the heart monitor machine. Gabriella slept, sitting on a chair with her head and arms draped across Vicente's chest. She slowly stirred as she realized she needed to scratch an itch on her arm.

As Gabriella lifted her head, she was met with a painful stiff neck. She let out a slight groan, reaching behind her head to massage the kink out. She looked down at her watch that now showed it close to 5 o'clock.

Gabriella's stomach growled, plus she suffered from a slight headache. She hadn't eaten since the blast and felt horrible, still wearing the same dirty clothes since the explosion. She needed to take a shower and check on Lucita.

Being the maternal mother and loving spouse, her attention had been so focused on taking care of Vicente that she allowed her own needs to fall to the wayside. In addition, her patience grew thin. She wanted answers from Ignacio on what happened, but he had not returned yet.

Gabriella also wondered why the hell Diego had not returned yet. Now gone for several hours, something did not make sense. As she sat by Vicente's side throughout the night, he had not moved, he laid there resting comfortably.

One of the metal doors gently swung open. Gabriella turned in her chair to see the doctor walking into the room, carrying a hot cup of coffee. He looked at Gabriella and smiled. "How is our patient doing?"

"He hasn't moved at all."

"That is good, very good. Here, I brought this for you," he said, handing her the coffee. "I thought you might need this."

Gabriella smiled. His kindness was exactly what she needed. "Thank you."

She took the cup of coffee, taking a slow sip from the steaming hot cup. The doctor walked around the table and bent down to examine the wound on Vicente's head. It seemed to be healing okay, although it still appeared quite red.

The doctor then turned his attention to Vicente's knee, it too still swollen, but looked slightly better than it did the day before. The doctor walked to the other side of the table, taking a glance at the heart monitoring machine. Vicente's blood pressure and pulse held steady. In fact, they improved dramatically.

The doctor leaned forward placing both hands on the table looking at Gabriella.

"He is doing very well. His wounds are healing, and his heart rate is strong. I think he is going to be okay."

Gabriella was relieved. She took in a deep breath and slowly exhaled. She placed her cup of coffee on the table, stood up and walked next to the table, looking across at the doctor.

"You have no idea what this man means to me. He is my everything. Thank you for taking such wonderful care of him. I will make sure you are taken care of when this is over."

Gabriella hadn't been humbled too many times in her life, in this moment however, it would be the exception.

"Señora De Los Santos, this is what I get paid to do. You need to do nothing more."

He reached over the table and placed his hand on Gabriella's shoulder in a reassuring gesture.

"I will be back a little later to check on him again." As he prepared to walk through the doors and exit the room, the metal doors slammed open, catching him off guard, forcing him to stumble backward. Gabriella spun to see Santino walking in her direction.

"Mamá!" he cried out.

"How is Papá?"

Santino suppressed many emotions why he didn't like his father, sometimes he even hated him. Most notably he was a heinous drug lord that murdered people but, at the end of the day, that was still his dad.

"Santino, mi hijo, you're here! How did you get here?"

Gabriella now overcome with emotion. She teared up as she looked at her son. She had not seen him in several months. Santino and Gabriella rushed to each other and embraced. Much taller than his mother, he wrapped his strong arms around her waist to hug her, lifting her off the floor. He, too, was overcome with emotion and started to tear up.

As his mother hugged him back, he looked down at his father laying on the table. Unable to comprehend the condition his father was in. All his life, he remembered his father to be indestructible, nearly a mythic figure, but for the first time, he witnessed his father as weak and wounded.

Gabriella took a step back, placing her hands-on Santino's face.

"What are you doing here?"

Santino observed the tears running down his mother's face and tried to wipe away the sadness with his hands.

"Please, Mamá, don't cry. I am here now, that is all that matters." Santino hugged her once again, looking back down at his unconscious father. He walked around to the other side of the table. Santino grasped his father's hand into his, holding it gently but firmly. He could never think of a time in his life when his father or his family appeared so wounded and vulnerable.

"How did this happen?"

Gabriella looked over at him.

"It was an explosion. It happened during Lucita's party. I don't know anything more than that right now. I've been with your father the entire night."

"At Lucita's birthday party? At my baby sister's birthday party?" Santino sounded confused and disgusted at the same time.

"Yes," Gabriella nodded.

"I heard the explosion, at my game, the entire stadium did. It's all over the news. I've been trying to reach all of you, but no one will answer their damn phones! I borrowed a friend's car and came as quickly as I could. I stopped by the house, but it is swarming with police and reporters. So, I came here. I figured all of you had to be here."

"Oh, honey, your soccer game. I forgot all about it. How did you do?"

"We won Mamá, but that's not important right now, I will share that with you later. Where is Lucita? Is she okay?"

Gabriella smiled. She knew how much Santino loved his little sister and what she meant to him.

"She is fine. She is upstairs sleeping."

"How is Papá? Is he going to be okay?" Santino asked, still staring down at his father.

The doctor still in the room during the exchange waited quietly, finally taking his turn to speak.

"Your father is going to be okay, Santino. He arrived with some nasty injuries, but I fixed him all up. He needs some rest now."

Santino, embarrassed that he hadn't noticed the doctor as he rushed right past him when he barged into the room, walked around the table over to where the doctor stood. Santino paused a moment, smiled, and wrapped his arms around him, giving him a vice-like bear hug.

The doctor let out a brief chuckle and gasped for air. Santino released his grip, placing his hands on the doctor's shoulders.

"Dr. Mendoza, I wouldn't have entrusted my father to anyone but you. I'm glad to see you."

Dr. Mendoza served as the lifelong private family doctor to the De Los Santos family. Vicente paid him handsomely to be on twenty-four-hour call for the family. Throughout the years, though, he generally had been called upon for minor things such as cuts and scrapes when Santino and Ignacio would get into fistfights.

Vicente trusted Dr. Mendoza because they grew up together in the same poor neighborhood. When Vicente started his rise to power and ultimately gained control, Dr. Mendoza expressed his loyalty to Vicente, even though he had many opportunities to betray him. Vicente never had to doubt the devotion to his family. Dr. Mendoza smiled at Santino.

"It is terrific to see you too, Santino. You look well."

They both stood there for a moment, enjoying the brief reunion. Santino remembered all the kindness Dr. Mendoza showed him over the years. In the midst of wrapping up their heartfelt moment, the metal doors once again swung open. Ignacio rushed into the room. His appearance was disheveled, sweaty and dirty.

He, too, still wearing the same dingy, tattered clothes as the day before. As he entered the room, Ignacio immediately layed eyes on his mother standing at his father's side as he lay motionless on the table. What an incredibly a good sign for Ignacio; he knew his father had not been asking questions at this point.

Wasting no time Gabriella jumped right in,

"Where the hell have you been?" she barked at him.

"I've been here all-night waiting for an update from you. I need some answers." She stared directly into Ignacio's eyes, walking toward him until she positioned herself directly in front of him.

"Well, I'm waiting. Tell me what you've found."

She crossed her arms and planted her feet. Feeling no need to move until Ignacio explained himself. His mother someone he would never challenge. "And why the hell are you so dirty?" She shrieked, giving him no room to think.

Ignacio cleared his throat.

"Mamá, I have some terrible news. I . . . "

"Yes, *Ignacio*. Tell us what you found."

When he rushed into the room, Ignacio hadn't bothered to notice Santino and Dr. Mendoza standing next to the door. Recognizing the voice instantly, he turned his body around slow. Ignacio's eyes widened for a brief second; his body stiffened as he looked his brother standing there glaring at him. Santino walked toward him out of shadows, gazing at him.

The room very quickly became tense and exceptionally uncomfortable. The two brothers, still with a great deal of disdain for one another, harbored years of animosity and ill will over fights and betrayals. Each man considering the other as an embarrassment to the family. Santino perceived Ignacio as a weak bully, a man child, who always demanded his own way and killed to get it.

Ignacio viewed Santino as a traitor that abandoned his family, a weak little boy who ran away the first chance he got, in essence a coward. Both brothers close in physical stature, muscular and strong, but mentally, they were miles apart. Santino continued his passive taunt.

"Go ahead and tell us what you found, *brother*." Santino highly aware that whatever Ignacio was about to say would be complete bullshit.

"What I have to say doesn't concern you, asshole." Ignacio snapped back. "What the hell gives you the right to question me or ask me anything? Where the hell were you? Where the hell have you been this whole time?"

Santino, never the one to back down, leaned in closer to Ignacio.

"Where the hell was I pendejo? Where the hell were you, Mr. Badass? Your one and only job is to protect your father and family, but you couldn't even do that!"

The two brothers stood locked in a death stare. If looks could kill, Gabriella would have lost both of her sons' right at that moment. Tired of the bickering, she interjected herself into their squabble.

"Oh, stop this shit, the both of you. Neither of you is to blame. We're here for your father, and that is all that matters."

Gabriella hated to be in the middle of her son's fight, understanding why they did however. All males in her life were alpha's, competing for dominance in their own way. The two brothers continued to glare at each other.

Finally, Ignacio broke his stare, letting out a sigh and looked over at his mother.

"What I have to tell you can wait, it needs to be done privately. I'm going up to check on Lucita."

Ignacio shot one last glance at Santino standing there, giving him a *fuck you* look. Gabriella, not pleased, opened her mouth and forced Ignacio to speak as he turned and made his way to the door.

Suddenly, as so many times previously, the metal doors flew open, this time pushing Ignacio backward.

"Well, well, well. Looks like the gang is all here!"

Santino, Gabriella, and Ignacio looked on in amazement. Ignacio's body tingled but not in a good way, anger seeped in. Gabriella watched with a confused expression on her face. Santino seemed to be the only one rather pleased to see Diego come walking into the room. He looked defeated, with Aurelio directly behind him with a big smile on his face.

Aurelio's placed his hand on Diego's shoulder as he walked him into the room. Diego made eye contact with no one. He looked down at the floor as he walked in, stopping feet away from Ignacio.

Ignacio stared at Diego with wrath in his eyes. Gabriella too angry he had brought him here. Santino walked toward his uncle without saying a word, both men embraced in a hug slapping each other in the back.

"Ah, nephew, it is good to see you again. I heard you won your soccer game yesterday, congratulations!"

Aurelio had a particular fondness for Santino. Mainly because he chose to take a completely different path in life and do some good in the world despite his family.

"Yes, we did, Uncle. It was amazing, but we can talk about that later. It is good to see you too!" Both men slapped each other on the shoulder. Aurelio turned and looked at Gabriella.

"Hello, Gabriella, how is my brother doing?"

"He is doing fine as you can see. What the hell are you doing here? What's going on?"

Gabriella starting to get annoyed by his presence. Aurelio chuckled,

"Man, it's nice to see you too." sounding sarcastic.

Aurelio continuing his moment of sarcasm looked at Ignacio.

"Hello, Nephew. Kill anyone lately?"

Ignacio felt his emotions building up but kept his cool. He turned to his mother, and in a soft but unsettling tone, said,

"I am going upstairs to check on Lucita." He wanted out of the room.

Aurelio, never being the one for letting an opportunity pass him by, blurted out,

"Whoa, you don't want to hang out with us for a bit? I've got some juicy facts to share about my investigation."

Ignacio realized his uncle was trying to bait him still, he wondered how much did he know? And what did he and Diego speak of? Maybe Aurelio was only guessing at this point, empty theories, to see if Ignacio would break. Maybe feed him some dis-information and bullshit to see what he'd do. Ignacio was willing to take the chance. He walked over to the desk and sat down, crossing his legs. Putting on a fake smile, he looked at Aurelio and calmly said,

"It's your world, Uncle, I'm just living in it," reeking of sarcasm.

Not missing a beat, Aurelio shot back,

"That's right and don't forget it."

Aurelio strolled over to where Vicente was laying. He stared down at his brother for a moment.

"Damn, they did a number on you, Hermano."

He tapped the table twice with his knuckle, spinning around to visualize the entire room. He realized Dr. Mendoza still standing in the room watching the fireworks take place. "Dr. Mendoza, you're free to go, sir."

Dr. Mendoza said nothing, nodding his head and departing.

"Man, what a day. What a night." Aurelio said. "Busy, busy, busy. I have been up now for . . . seventeen hours. I have scoured every single inch of your home and have found some pretty interesting stuff. First, though, let me say fifteen people are dead. Eight of them children."

He paused for a moment to let the horror of the statement sink in. The room fell somber, even Ignacio lowered his head to ponder his mistake. Aurelio continued, pointing at Diego,

"You can thank your boy over there for bringing me here. I insisted on seeing my family, not knowing, of course, whether you would all be here. But I really didn't give him much of an option." He paused again as he watched Diego nervously shift his weight from one foot to another.

"Seems like whoever did this targeted some pretty big fish. Perhaps the Junta Directiva. That takes some enormous balls."

Aurelio struck a hard glance over at Ignacio.

"I don't have names of all the deceased as of yet. However, I expect them to roll through any moment. What's more interesting . . . and what I can't seem to wrap my mind around is, why would someone use nitroglycerin?"

"Nitroglycerin?" Gabriella snapped. "How the hell do you know that? And who the hell would do this?"

Aurelio chuckled once again, looking over at Gabriella.

"I'm pretty good at what I do. I think my team is pretty smart too. But, since we are asking questions here, let me ask you a question. Why the bullshit guest list? Your delivery boy over there brought me your little list of ten people. From looking at the security camera footage, there had to be easily a hundred people there."

Aurelio paused but didn't break his stare with Gabriella.

"I could not possibly remember the names of over a hundred people," she shot back.

"I gave you a list of those that I remembered, that was it."

Aurelio still looking to taunt and poke at her a little responded,

"Hmm, really. Wow, so you miraculously forget to mention that the Junta Directiva attended your party? Interesting. The most powerful men in all of Mexico, and you didn't notice them?"

By this time, Gabriella appeared annoyed and definitely not in any mood to answer any more questions.

"I don't have time for this. I've not eaten, and I feel like crap. I'm going to go and check on Lucita. You know where the door is, you can find your way out."

And with that, she stormed out of the room. Aurelio undoubtedly struck a nerve with Gabriella. And in his typical police interrogation fashion realized he was in complete control of the situation. He repositioned himself at the end of the table next to Vicente's head to get a better view at his wound.

"Man, that looks nasty."

He paused again before saying anything more.

He thrived in moments like this, letting the suspense build, making people around him uncomfortable. Santino the only one in the room not nervous, chimed in.

"Uncle, not to be rude," "But how do you know it was nitroglycerin? That's some major stuff."

"My bomb-sniffing dogs. And the crime scene technicians. You're right, that is some major stuff. Which leads me back to my original theory, perhaps someone tried to assassinate Junta Directiva." Aurelio replied.

Aurelio moved over to where Ignacio sat, trying to appear calm. Aurelio sat on the edge of the desk, flashing him a smirky stare, overtly bumping his leg with his shoe.

"You wouldn't happen to know anyone that would want to take out the entire Board of Directors and gain exclusive control of your family business, would you?"

Ignacio uncrossed his legs and leaned forward.

"Nope!"

Then leaned back in the chair. Ignacio's arrogance always bothered Aurelio, but this time it really began to piss him off, so he decided to turn up the heat. Aurelio got up from the desk and walked back to the table, this time keeping his back to Ignacio.

"Don't suppose you have any knowledge about the other explosion that happened last night, down at an old warehouse in the slums. They found a body inside."

Diego shifted his body to now stand behind Ignacio. He glanced down at him, knowing that he had gotten to the bomb maker. Ignacio stared at the back of his uncle's police vest, once again responding,

"Nope."

La Familia: Loose Ends

Aurelio turned and locked eyes with Ignacio. Now ready for the kill shot, Aurelio tipped his hand,

"Okay, smart guy. It seems like you don't know a lot about anything. So, I wonder if you know the guy that drove the bomb to your house. The one I captured on the security video. I also wonder if you know I have your boy, Diego, shaking hands with that same asshole when he gets there."

Aurelio paused, closing his eyes tapping his finger on his forehead,

"Oh yeah, I almost forgot, the same dumb ass, your boy standing behind you, hands him an envelope full of money that he just happened to have on him. "

Aurelio stopped one last time, snapping his fingers letting out a lighthearted laugh.

" Oh yeah and I also wonder if you know that I was able to get the license plate off that white van as it drove off."

Aurelio reached into his pocket, pulling out his notepad.

"G-F-H-2-9-8-7. It seems like I know more than you, *Nephew*." Aurelio tucked the notepad back into his pocket. He stood there fully knowing he just poked the bear and waited for Ignacio's response. The attitudes in the room had shifted. Aurelio dripped with bravado and swagger. Whereas Ignacio now sat there without his brazen, cocky smile.

His looked distant, aggravated, he felt about ready to come out of his skin. Everything Aurelio talked about had been the stone-cold truth. Ignacio realized his uncle was close to figuring this thing out, and on the inside, Ignacio was dying. How could Diego have been so stupid to get caught on camera with the driver of the van?

But was he really surprised? After all, he'd been out cleaning up Diego's messes all night. However, this potentially was the smoking gun.

Ignacio held it together, everything depended on it. He could not get sucked in by his uncle's attempts to get a rise out of him.

Ignacio stood up, briefly eyeballing Diego. Diego recognized that look and knew there would be no good to come from it. Ignacio walked over to Aurelio. As much as he hated his uncle, he understood the consequences of striking a police officer. Ignacio taking in a controlled breath finally spoke.

"I guess you do know more than me, Uncle."

He stepped to the side of Aurelio and bent down to kiss his father on his head, an empty gesture, but he still had to keep up appearances. Ignacio turned and walked over to Santino, giving him an icy glare. As he exited the room, Gabriella came walking through the door again, this time holding Lucita's hand. Lucita's little face lit up with a big smile as she saw both Aurelio and Santino standing there. She rushed toward Aurelio as he bent down on one knee to hug her.

"Uncle Aurelio, I am so happy to see you!"

Lucita wrapped her arms around his neck and squeezed tight, holding onto him as if he might disappear forever. He held her around her waist and smiled at her. This one little girl brought him a lot of joy and happiness in his life, and he was glad she felt safe in his arms.

"I am so delighted to see you too, Lucita, sweetheart. I am pleased to see you are okay."

Aurelio held her at arm's length to get a good look at her face. She indeed looked like she had been through the worst experience of her life. On the inside, he went from happy to angry. He thought about how close she came to dying and how this would affect her for the rest of her life.

"Here, let me look at you sweetheart. How are you feeling?"

Aurelio brushed her hair out of her face and touched her cheek. His eyes glazed over with tears, so thankful to have her standing before him.

"I am okay, Uncle. I mean, I am not hurt at least, but my friends, some of them died."

Lucita's eyes filled with tears as she looked down at the floor. The gravity of what she experienced affected her again. Aurelio pulled her back into his arms, wrapping her up with a hug of pure love and understanding.

"I know, sweetheart, it was such a rough day for you. Have you had something to eat?" Lucita nodded.

Gabriella cleared her throat and spoke up.

"I went upstairs to check on her, and she was awake. I told her you were all down here, and she insisted on seeing you. I couldn't have stopped her if I wanted to."

Santino stepped from behind the table, walking up directly behind Aurelio. He looked down at Lucita as she buried her face in Aurelio's shoulder. Santino smiled and placed his hand on her shoulder.

"Don't I get a hug?"

Lucita looked up and smiled as Aurelio released her from a hug. She took a step toward forward into her big brother's arms, hugging him. Santino scooped her up, holding her tight. He, too, was happy to see his baby sister unharmed. The two stood there for a moment, holding each other tight their arms. Not saying a word, cherishing this moment of bliss in his heart.

Everyone in the room watched them embrace, each of them realizing how close she had come to being killed. Finally, Santino put his little sister down, kneeling beside her.

"I am so sorry this happened to you, Lucita, but you know that our uncle will find who is responsible for this and bring them to justice."

Lucita nodded.

"If Uncle Aurelio does not find them, will Papá?"

The question caught Santino a bit off guard. He said nothing at first, knowing in his heart that his father would absolutely avenge this matter. When Vicente discovered who was responsible for this, there would likely be a level of savagery that no one had seen before. Aurelio placed his hand on her shoulder, flashing a bright smile.

"When your father wakes up from his rest, he is only going to want to know that you are okay. I will find out who did this, I promise you."

"Okay, Lucita," Gabriella said.

"I want you to go back upstairs and take a shower and change into some clean clothes. It's time you got out of that dress; the adults need to talk. I'll be up to check on you shortly."

Lucita hugged Santino and Aurelio once more, soon after walking out of the room, leaving Gabriella, Santino, Ignacio, Aurelio, and Diego to all stare at each other. The room filled with awkward silence.

Finally, Aurelio turned to Santino.

"Nephew, it is good seeing you. I will stop by later to catch up. Maybe you can tell me about your soccer game?"

Santino smiled.

"Oh, of course, Uncle. I will be waiting."

Aurelio looked over at Gabriella.

"I don't have to tell you how serious this is. You're going to need to give me something more than a bullshit guest list," his voice was stern.

"I will be in touch." Aurelio looked at Ignacio.

"Don't you go too far. I might have some questions for you." Ignacio nodded his head. Aurelio lastly looked over at Diego, who still stood by the desk.

"And you, thanks for the conversation. We'll talk later!"

Diego couldn't believe it. Aurelio had just signed his death warrant. Gabriella looked at Diego in disbelief. Ignacio's look was clear. *I am going to kill you.*

Aurelio winked at Diego, pushed his way out of the room, and headed out to his car. Santino could tell there was friction between his mother, Ignacio, and Diego. Still, he was too tired and too hungry to get involved. He turned around to lay a small kiss on his father's forehead, then looked at his mother,

"I'm going to go upstairs and eat and keep Lucita company." Afterward, giving her a gentle hug. He threw glances at both Diego and Ignacio and headed for the door. Suddenly they all heard a loud gasp. The sound scared everyone in the room. They turned to witness Vicente roll slightly to one side in an attempt to catch his breath. He began coughing, they looked at one another in shock. Vicente was starting to awaken!

Chapter 8: Worlds Collide

When Aurelio arrived at the scene of the explosion, he couldn't help but think it felt like déjà vu. Another location had suffered a devastating blast with potentially more casualties, along with the chaos of lights, cops, and the news media running around. Aurelio deemed his odds to be fairly high that dead body waiting inside would be his bomb maker, considering that the explosion had been powerful enough to level three buildings.

He parked his vehicle away from the mayhem just in case he needed to make a quick exit. Before exiting, he sat in his car for a moment, staring at the steering wheel, tapping his foot on the floor. Something just didn't sit right with him playing back in his mind the conversations and exchanges with Ignacio, Diego, and Gabriella.

Aurelio's instincts had been screaming at him from the time he left. Sensing someone in that group knew something, but they obviously weren't saying anything. Part of him understood that their screwed-up code of never talking to the police and handle everything within the family. He would always be an outsider looking in as long as he wore the badge.

This time, however, there seemed to be something deeply wrong, something sinister. Ignacio displayed a cockier attitude more brazen than usual. He seemed to taunt Aurelio, as if to say, *I know something you don't, and you'll never find out.* Aurelio now seriously questioned himself. Could his own nephew, his own flesh and blood, have such contempt for his family to do something like this?

Ignacio was raised to be a killer, and to kill at all costs, especially if it meant preserving power and respect for the family. But this attack displayed a whole new level of evil and inhumane behavior.

Could Ignacio be cold enough to want to kill his mother, father, baby sister, and the Junta Directiva?

If Aurelio were honest with himself, the answer had to be yes. If Ignacio's path and rise to power mirrored anything close to his father's, it meant killing anyone in his way. Perhaps Gabriella and Lucita unfortunately had become pawns or collateral damage. Nonetheless, now everyone was intertwined in this sadistic plot. And then there is Diego.

He was a dumb ass, sloppy, not as well connected, but in his bones, Aurelio had no doubts he had something to do with it. After all, he saw him on video shaking hands with the van driver. Aurelio needed to figure out how to make all the pieces fit. Aurelio started to feel the mental strain from being up so long.

He sat straight up and started shaking his head, slapping his face, letting out small grunts and growls. Aurelio needed to wake himself up a little more and get out of this tired daze. He needed to get his mind focused before he walked into the next war zone. Immediately before he got out, he reached down and grabbed his police radio, turning the small black dials to channel three, a restricted channel, and called out to his sergeant.

"Sergeant Ramos, come in." There was a brief pause, then he chimed in.

"This is Ramos. Go."

"How are we in the investigation at the house?" Aurelio asked.

"We're okay here, just about wrapped up."

"Good. I need you to run a license plate for me and get back to me quickly, this is time sensitive. G-F-H-2-9-8-7, it should be connected to a white passenger van."

"Copy that G-F-H-2-9-8-7 I'm on it right now. Anything else, Lieutenant?"

"Negative, this is for my ears only, though. When you find out about it, get back to me and no one else got it?

"Yep, copy that. I will get right back to you. Ramos out."

Aurelio knew he had to get his hands on that van; it meant the key to everything. He wanted to handle the van on his own, though. If there was a chance someone from his family, or connected to his family, may have been involved, he needed to get a hold of that information first.

Aurelio pushed opened his car door and was hit with an immediate foul stench of rotten eggs, wet dog, and spoiled fish. His stomach, not ready, started churning right away feeling so caught off guard, he wondered if he might even throw up. The rancid smell of burning bricks mixed with the chemical reaction of all the explosives and firefighting foam filled the air with a repulsive odor that even a seasoned veteran had trouble handling.

He walked to the back of his police car and opened the trunk. He reached inside, locating a small black duffel bag. Retrieving a face mask, he placed it across his mouth and nose, hooking the elastic bands around his ears to help block out the repulsive stench. He began his walk toward the commotion of the fire trucks and news media.

As usual, the news reporters started yelling questions at him as he walked by. They flashed their lights and pushed their microphones in his face as they attempted to ask a never-ending barrage of questions. They were roped off far enough away that they couldn't follow him, but they were annoying, nonetheless. Aurelio put his hands up to shield his eyes from their bright lights.

"No comment!" he barked as he walked past them.

When he cleared the media circus, he came to a small group of residents from the neighborhood, standing around watching the action. He secretly hoped there may be a witness or two in the crowd.

All the nearby buildings that survived the blast had shattered front windows. It was a poor neighborhood, so they didn't have much to begin with, but maybe someone destroying their block would piss them off enough to want to speak up.

"Lieutenant De Los Santos, over here!" a man screamed.

Aurelio looked over to his right, noticing a man standing on an immense pile of rubble, waving his arms. Plumes of white smoke still rose from the piles of brick all around him. Aurelio made his way over to the Commander, climbing up the mound of debris. The bricks and pieces of masonry shifted underneath him with each step he took.

The nauseating smells grew worse in this area. Aurelio attempted to press the mask tighter around his nose and mouth with one hand, as he maintained his balance with the other arm. It wasn't working well. He finally reached the top of the pile where the fire commander stood.

"It's not very flattering, is it?" the Commander asked.

"No, it's not. So, what do you have for me?"

"So far, one dead. Male. Gunshot wound to the back of the head. I can't believe we're not dealing with more bodies considering the size of the explosion."

"Where is the body? I want to see it."

"Follow me." The Commander swung his arm for Aurelio to follow. They traveled a short distance, with Commander Alvarez pointing to a white sheet on the ground a few yards away.

"Right there, that's your guy. I'm gonna stay right here. Hope you don't mind, but I don't fare well around dead bodies."

"No, not a problem at all. Let me ask you, though, is this where you found him?"

"Yes and no. After we put out a majority of the fire, we made our way to this side to see if we needed to continue our efforts. One of my men lost his footing and slipped unearthing him. It scared the shit out of him."

Alvarez chuckled slightly.

"We removed some of the bricks around him. I figure we're standing on the second floor right now. When we exposed enough of the body, or what's left of him, we covered him with the white sheet."

"So, no one ever physically moved or tampered with the body?" Aurelio asked.

"No, sir, what you see is what you get."

"Okay, good, thank you."

Aurelio took a few more steps down the pile of rubble to get a better look at the mysterious body under the white sheet. Glancing down at his watch, it was now almost 6 o'clock. As he kneeled down beside the body, the rising sun caught his eye. It just started to break over the mountaintops, exposing the exquisite beauty of the jungle off in the distance.

He stared out into the sky, looking far beyond the insanity of the moment. The sun felt good on his face, he closed his eyes for a few seconds. Regardless of how ghastly the smell was around him, he transcended the moment, away from what he would witness. He opened his eyes again, looking down at the white sheet, then he reached down and grabbed a small corner, pulling it back.

A bullet to the back of the head seemed apparent. Considering the guy was missing a sizeable portion of the front of his skull. The man's body had endured horrific burns with his right leg being blown off at mid-thigh. Most of his fingers had melted, and once again, the smell was overpowering, but this time the aroma was simply burned flesh.

As Aurelio examined the body, he did not gain much from it. Not even able to guess his age due to the extensive damage.

The only hope he had for identifying the remains would come from the dental records. That's if this guy had ever gone to the dentist. The only thing he understood for sure, this guy unquestionably did not shoot himself in the head, so that definitely made it murder. Still, without a positive identification, or a murder weapon, he had just hit another dead end. As he stood back up, his cell phone rang. He reached inside his front vest pocket and quickly pulled it out.

"Hello, Lieutenant Del Los Santos."

"Lieutenant, this is the chief medical examiner. I have a positive ID on a few of those bodies for you. There's one in particular I thought you might want to know about right away. I hope you're sitting down."

"I'm not but go ahead anyway, I'm ready."

"I've been able to positively identify one of the eight children through dental records." The medical examiner paused, "Alejandra Rivera."

Aurelio felt dizzy, as if he had just been punched in the stomach. He sensed his blood pressure fluctuating, he needed to steady himself. It was taking everything in his power not to collapse. He couldn't believe what he heard.

"Lieutenant, are you still there? Did you hear me?" The medical examiner asked.

Aurelio still stuck in his thoughts quickly snapped out of his daze.

"No. I heard you thank you."

Hanging up and ending their call. Aurelio's arm dropped to his side, digesting the devastating news. He looked down at all the activity around the scene. Everything seemed so far away.

All the noise and commotion sounded muffled. His eyes glazed over; his chest swelled with emotional pain. Never in his career did the news about a child's death get any easier, but this was different. This information had just given birth to the worst possible scenario because this was no regular child. Alejandra Rivera was the daughter of Felix Rivera, one of the bosses who sat on the Junta Directiva, and Lucita's best friend.

Felix Rivera earned a reputation for being a merciless tyrant with little room for understanding under normal conditions. He had come close to running Junta Directiva in the war against Vicente before the board had been established. Vicente proved to be a more cunning adversary and murderer, annihilating all of Felix's supply and distribution chains, forcing him into submission.

This was Felix's only child—his pride and joy—now she had been ruthlessly murdered. Aurelio knew Felix. When he found out, all bets would be off, and an all-out war would ensue. In an instant, Aurelio called the medical examiner back. The phone rang and rang.

"C'mon, pick up the damn phone."

Finally, the medical examiner answered.

"Have you told the parents yet, have you told anyone?"

Aurelio shouted.

The medical examiner surprised responded promptly.

"No, I've said nothing to no one."

Aurelio breathing a sigh of relief,

"Good. Don't say a damn thing to anyone. You keep this and any other information you have under wraps until I give you the okay to release it. Got it?"

Aurelio's tone sounded fierce. He realized the damage this would cause, and he needed to control its release.

"I understand. I thought you might think that way, so I am the only one with this knowledge for now."

"Good, thank you," Aurelio relaxed his tone.

"I will contact you when we can go public with this."

Aurelio ended the call and contemplated his next move. The dead body laying at his feet presented no more answers, and now the ante had just been raised. Just as he made his way back down the stack of smoldering bricks and wreckage, his phone rang once again. He looked down at his phone and saw the name Ramos appear.

"Sergeant Ramos, I hope you have located that van and have some good news for me."

Sergeant Ramos moaned slightly, "Well, we know who the van belongs to, but you may not find it to be great news. The tag comes back registered to a chop shop down on the lower south side. After doing some digging, Lieutenant, well, the owner of the chop shop is your nephew, Ignacio."

Aurelio's eyes grew wide, and his heart started racing, he blurted out, "Get some of our men down there right now. Get eyes on that fucking location but tell them to stay back until I get there and send me the address of that fucking chop shop. I'm on my way!"

Aurelio couldn't believe it. This was incredible. This very well might be the smoking gun that tied Ignacio to the attack and would put his ass away. Aurelio stuffed his phone back in his pocket and began making his way back down to the street. A minute later, his phone started vibrating.

He took a quick glance at it, realizing Ramos had sent him the address. He saw Commander Alvarez and hollered at him, "You can have the body taken away, Commander. I'm done with it. I have to go. There's something else I need to attend to."

Alvarez waved in acknowledgment as Aurelio jogged back to his vehicle, managing this time to bypass the crowd of reporters. He reached his cruiser, removed his mask, throwing it down on the ground. He got in the car, turned on his lights and sirens, whipped his car around and took off, headed for Ignacio's chop shop.

<u>Chapter 9: The High Art of Lying</u>

They all stood there in stunned disbelief, staring at him, their mouths ajar. After what seemed like an eternity, Vicente was waking up. Gabriella, the first one to rush over to his side, started stroking his hair.

"Sweetheart, I am here." She grabbed his hand and gently caressed his head.

"Breath my sweetheart . . . just breathe." Vicente coughed, slightly gasping for air, trying to sit up, still somewhat disorientated. Gabriella turned to Santino.

"Go and get him some water." Santino nodded and rushed out of the room.

"Honey, please, take it easy, and relax, don't try to sit up."

Vicente laid back down, opening his eyes, staring up at the ceiling. He reached his hand up to rub his head, finding the large bandage over his wound. His breathing still labored.

"How long have I been out? He asked, struggling to get the words out.

"For a long while, my love. It's been close to eighteen hours, I imagine. I have been here this whole time with you. We're all okay."

"My mouth is dry. I need some water or ice," he said with a whisper.

"It's on the way, we'll have it in a moment, my love, relax."

Diego and Ignacio both stood there watching. They said nothing but locked eyes with each other, knowing that the timing of this had accelerated everything. Ignacio realized he reached the point of no return and had to put his plan into motion if he stood any chance of spinning this mess in his favor.

While staring at Diego, he motioned to him with a subtle head nod to leave the room. Diego agreed and began to make his way to the door. Santino returned, bursting through the doors with a large pitcher of water and a glass.

"Get out of my way," he barked at Diego.

Diego shuffled to the side, holding the door, allowing Ignacio to walk out, closely trailing behind him.

After they moved into the hallway, Ignacio silently motioned for Diego to follow him placing his finger to his lips, gesturing for him to be quiet. Ignacio turned and headed down the hallway toward their secret meeting room, where they had spoken the day before. As Ignacio turned the corner, Diego wondered if this would be the last time he would come out of this room alive.

After they walked past the tall spiral staircase, they stood in front of an enormous concrete statue of an Aztec warrior. Ignacio looked around to make sure no one had followed them. Realizing that the coast was clear, Ignacio reached behind the back of the large statue and pushed a button. The large concrete statue released from its position, exposing the secret room.

After they both had entered, Ignacio pulled the statue back into place, closing the panel and concealing the room. Diego found himself in a familiar and unsettling position once again, alone, in trouble, and in the room with his best friend, a heartless killer. Ignacio walked up to Diego, saying nothing, looking him in the eyes.

Diego stood there ready for anything, not sure what would happen. His fists clenched, his forehead sweating, and his jaw tense. Ignacio planted his feet, staring at him. Finally, he placed his hand on Diego's shoulder.

"Look, we need to get to that van before my uncle does. I don't care what has happened up to this point. With my uncle, or you being on that video. I don't care what you might have said to him. I know you would not betray me, but if he finds that van, we're both done."

Diego gave a slight sigh of relief, although still skeptical about what Ignacio might do. He grew uncertain on what to think.

"I didn't mean to get sucked in by your uncle. I told him nothing. All that bullshit in the room earlier he's trying to make me look bad. I swear, I told him nothing."

Ignacio stepped back and walked past him.

"Like I said, I'm not worried about any of that right now. I understand how my uncle can be. He's sneaky and manipulative. You saw how he attempted to bait me? And besides, do you think if I thought you had told him anything, you and I would be standing here right now? All I care about is getting that van. Where is it?"

Ignacio already knew the answer to the question because of Jaguar's confession, however, he wanted to hear it from Diego himself. Diego turned to face Ignacio, not comfortable having his back to him. He was having a hard time reading Ignacio. He stood there for a second or two, observing him.

"It's back at the chop shop. It's scheduled to be dismantled today."

Astonished by Diego's honesty but not so much by his stupidity, nothing surprised Ignacio anymore. The fact that the van currently sat on his property was typical of Diego's sloppiness. Ignacio now in full clean-up mode had no reservation s, any and all loose ends, which now included his best friend, had to be dealt with. Diego had to go.

"Okay, here's what I need you to do. Go and get the van out of there right now. Take it and torch it. I don't care where you do it, just get rid of it. By now, my uncle has to be looking into it. If we're lucky, we can get to it before he does."

"What about your mother and father?" Diego asked.

"Don't worry about them right now. I'll cover for you. I'll tell them I told you to start making pickups and checking in with everyone. We still need to run the business. By now, there's talk on the streets, and people are wondering if our family is still intact. We need to show them we're still in power and that my father is okay. If anyone out there is going to try to test us, it will be now. We can't look weak."

Ignacio's' explanation seemed to make perfect sense, and Diego looking to redeem himself was all in. He wanted to make amends for his string of failures and do well this time. He needed to come through for Ignacio.

Ignacio took a step forward, placing his hand on Diego's shoulder in a reassuring gesture.

"Hey, c'mon, let's get moving. We can talk about anything else later once we have this mess cleaned up."

Diego cracked a slight smile, feeling as if he were no longer in the deep end of the pool drowning, but rather only up to his neck treading water. Before he walked out of the room, Ignacio gave him one last set of instructions.

"When you've taken care of the van, call me right away. I'll have you start making pickups and checking in with our street crews. This will solidify our story with my parents."

Diego nodded and made his way to the door. He pushed the button to release the statue, poking his head out to make sure no one was standing at the metal staircase or walking down the hallway. Realizing the coast was clear, he walked out with Ignacio following behind him.

Ignacio pushed the statue back into place, once again concealing the room. As Diego and Ignacio walked down the hallway, they slowed their pace, pausing before they passed by the doors that led to the infirmary, where Santino, Gabriella, and Vicente were. Ignacio peeked inside, seeing his mother still sitting by his father's side, comforting him.

Ignacio motioned for Diego to walk past him.

"Remember to call me immediately after you've gotten rid of the van."

And with that, Ignacio gave Diego a slight pat on the shoulder. Diego nodded, turned around, and left. Ignacio watched him walk down the hallway, knowing things would have to be perfectly executed for his plan to work. Unfortunately, for Diego, it would be at his expense. When he could no longer see Diego, Ignacio walked back into the infirmary to see his father taking small sips of water. He slowly made his way over to him. He walked up behind his mother and placed a hand on her shoulder.

"Papá, how do you feel?"

"I feel like shit, asshole. What do you think?"

Santino smiled. What a stupid question to ask. Seeing his opportunity to one-up his brother, Santino chimed into the conversation.

"Papá, take it easy. You're still in shock, your body is still suffering from the trauma. It's going to be awhile before you are one hundred percent. Please try to relax."

Vicente stopped rubbing his forehead long enough to look up. The bright light from the lamp above him was semi-blinding, so he could not see Santino's face. Vicente reached up, pushing the lamp away, to get a clear look at his magnificent son's face. He lifted his head up off the table, reaching over to grab Santino's hand and smiled.

"My son, you are here."

His tone sounding grateful, something that did not happen very often. He reached across his body with his other hand, grabbing Santino's forearm. "It is good to see you."

Santino looked down at his father with a smile, patting his father gently on the shoulder, reassuring him.

"It is good to see you too, Papá, I have missed you."

La Familia: Loose Ends

Vicente laid his head back down on the table. Ignacio stood there with contempt for his brother, thinking once again, the choir boy, the perfect angel. A brief moment of silence that filled the room. Ignacio saw his opportunity to put his plan in motion.

"Mamá, I need to speak with you," he whispered.

"Can't it wait, Ignacio? Your father just woke up. I should be here with him."

"No, I must really speak with you" he said, now with a sense of urgency in his voice.

Vicente barged his way into the conversation.

"What is it? What do you need to tell your mother? Is it about the attack? Do you have any information? Wounded or not, I am still the head of this family, not you! You're too mentally weak to lead. I demand that you tell me what is going on!"

Vicente suddenly sat up on the table, pushing his legs over the side. He used Santino as an anchor to pull himself up, grunting in pain from his damaged ribs. Before Gabriella or Santino could object or tell him no, he sat on the edge of the table looking at Ignacio. Blood vessels in Vicente's left eye were ruptured, making the whites of his eye red, giving him an even more depraved appearance.

Ignacio froze. He hadn't expected his father to react so aggressively.

"What the hell do you know? Speak up!"

Vicente snapped. In an instant, Ignacio had been brought back down to reality. Very rudely reminded why his father was the head of the family and why he hated him so much. Ignacio flashed Santino a quick glance, wishing he weren't in the room. Nonetheless, he would have to improvise and give the performance of a lifetime.

He stood up straight, placed his hands in his pockets, taking in a deep breath, letting out an exhale. The stalling only pissed Vicente off more.

"Speak the fuck up already, or I'm gonna put a bullet in your skull. Hell, if you had been doing your job in the first place, none of this would have happened!"

Little did Vicente realize that this all had explicitly happened because of him. Finally, Ignacio spoke.

"After they brought you here yesterday, I left right away to start backtracking and chasing down clues, leads, and people. I have excellent reason to believe that Diego is behind this attack on our family. I heard with my own ears, from multiple sources on the street last night, that he has been saying he is fed up by the way he has been treated and thinks he can run our business better than we can. I learned last night that a few weeks ago, he hired a bomb maker to make the bomb that was used at Lucita's party. I was able to find an address and tracked the guy down. When I got there and attempted to confront him, he attacked me and started shooting at me. So, I put one in his leg and interrogated him. He told me Diego hired him to build the bomb. He said Diego wanted to be the next drug lord of Mexico. With us and Junta Directiva out of the way that would set everything in motion. I put the bomb maker down with a bullet to his skull and blew up his building. After that, I reviewed the video surveillance footage from our house before Aurelio had the chance to. I accessed it from my laptop. You can see Diego shaking hands with the guy that delivered the bomb to our house. I printed off a picture of the guy and started showing it around, and it led me to a guy named Jaguar. I found him at a nightclub, partying. He was wasted, but I was able to get him to talk, he told me Diego hired him to drive the van to our house and drop off a package. He said he didn't know he was delivering a bomb. I lured him away from the nightclub and let's just say he won't be making any more deliveries. When Aurelio was here and tipped his hand about what he found so far in the investigation, it confirmed what I already knew. Still, I couldn't say anything to Mamá with Diego in the room."

Vicente looked confused.

"What the hell do you mean when my brother was here?"

He yelled.

"He was here in this room?"

Vicente struggled to stand, placing his weight on his good leg.

Ignacio stepped back. Gabriella attempted to chime into the conversation.

"Yes, dear, we were going to tell you, but not until you were strong enough, healthy enough to take it all in."

Vicente looked over at Gabriella and seethed with anger. Usually, he never disrespected his wife, but this time he was outraged and infuriated at the thought of his cop brother being in the same room with him.

"I don't remember asking you a fucking thing! Keep quiet!"

He shouted as he pointed his finger at her.

Gabriella stood there in a state of shock and disbelief. In all their decades of marriage, Vicente had never spoken to her that way. He never had as much as raised his voice to his wife. Even though he was a heartless killer, he had always been respectful, kind, and loving with her, she was his queen.

Gabriella definitely never accepted such foul language or disrespect from anyone, especially him. In this one instance, though, she made an exception and conceded her feelings. Her husband had just woken up from an attempt on his life. He needed time to fathom and digest everything his son had told him. She stood there and said nothing.

She folded her arms around her waist, turned around, and walked away. Vicente refocused his attention back on Ignacio, mustering all the energy he could.

"My fucking brother was here? Who the hell brought him here? How did that happen?" Vicente screamed, still wobbling on his leg.

"Diego brought him here, father, we were all shocked. I am not sure how he ended up with him."

Once again, Gabriella reluctantly chimed back in.

"I gave Diego a list of ten children's names that attended our party to bring to Aurelio. I had to give your brother something. He was pressing me for information, so I gave him a bullshit list to throw him off for a little while. I told Diego he needed to drop it off and come right back, and not to speak with Aurelio. He didn't return until almost two hours after I sent him, and then he came back with him."

"That's not all," Ignacio interrupted.

"When I came back here to tell Mamá about what I found, Diego started acting funny when he got here. Maybe he was nervous about bringing Aurelio here. I don't know. A few minutes ago, I tried to confront him about everything, but he took off. Diego said he had to go and do some pickups and touch base with the street crews. I told him that shit could wait, but he insisted. It seemed like he didn't want to be around us or face us."

Vicente stood there on his one good leg and slumped back onto the table. Santino placed his hand on the back of his father's shoulder to help give him a little more support. Vicente's eyes locked open wide as he looked down at the floor. His breathing now turned into heavy panting, but time sounding more controlled, more regulated.

"Pinche Madre," he muttered under his breath with his teeth grinding together.

He tried to collect his thoughts as he processed everything Ignacio told him.

"Something does not make sense to me. How could he have pulled all this off on his own, and especially without you knowing? He is your number two man, right? So how did he make all of these moves without your knowledge?"

Ignacio answered quickly.

"Days leading up to the attack, he would disappear for an hour here or an hour there. I thought he was just making special collections. He always had an answer for everything. I never suspected he was planning something like this; otherwise, I would have brought this to your attention right away. The two men I killed—Diego associated with them through acquaintances from old neighborhoods he worked in. I guess he became comfortable approaching them. I'm not sure, but what I do know is that he is out there somewhere right now doing God knows what, maybe trying to clean up even more of his mess. I need to get out there and track him down."

 Santino hadn't said a word, taking in Ignacio's entire bullshit story. However, curiosity got the best of him, and he saw another opportunity to ruffle his brother's feathers.

"So, brother, just one question. How did you find the bomb maker in the first place? You said the picture of the van driver eventually led you to him, but how did you know where to find the bomb maker. You just got lucky?"

A hush fell over the room. Both Gabriella and Vicente turned their attention to Ignacio, waiting for him to respond. Typical Santino, Ignacio thought. Always wanting to make him look like the bad guy. This time, though, Ignacio was prepared to cover his tracks. He felt reluctant at first to answer his brother. Still, he realized in the interest of self-preservation, and to avoid raising any alarms with his father, he should.

"Not that I have to answer to you, but one of the cops I pay well to give me information came through. He was at our house during the investigation. He overheard a conversation about the bomb maker, and the type of bomb used. He called me with that information, and I went from there."

Not taking the time to digest or over think the general explanation of his son's story, Vicente's mind had been made up. He wanted blood at this point. He stood back up, hobbling over to Ignacio, grimacing with each step. Gabriella attempted to help steady him, but he waved her off. When he reached Ignacio, he tried to straighten up as best he could to show he was still firmly in command of his family.

"Go find him and bring him to me," he said, in the iciest voice he could muster. Ignacio nodded, turned, and left the room. His father had taken the bait, and now he had one last loose end to tie up. Diego.

As Ignacio walked through the big wooden doors and out to the parking area, the sun shined brightly. He could tell it was going to be another blistering day. It was still relatively early in the morning. Considering the heat was already stifling hot, it appeared to be another omen for what a pressure cooker this day and this situation would be.

Ignacio reached his car and hopped inside. His stomach now growled as hunger set in. He, too, had not eaten in a very long time and was now feeling the effects of it. Ignacio tore out of the driveway headed to start his final phase of cleaning up this mess.

Chapter 10: The Spider and The Fly

Aurelio sat in the alley a half block away from Ignacio's chop shop. He reached behind his passenger-side car seat, digging out a pair of binoculars he had tucked into a black mesh bag that hung from the headrest. As he sat and stared at the building in question, everything looked quiet. The morning was still early, only a few minor people walking their dogs looking at their phones. The neighborhood was composed of a mixture of commercial buildings, warehouses, and apartment buildings. Aurelio gazed out across the area hard but saw nothing odd. As he looked through his binoculars, a man's voice called out to him on the radio.

"Lieutenant, are you there?"

"I'm here, what's up?" Aurelio replied.

"All seems quiet, not a lot of activity. How do you want to proceed? Are we even certain that the van's inside?"

Considering the street had only one way in or one way out, and they had eyes on it from every conceivable direction. If it was in there, it was definitely not getting out. This was a huge break in the investigation, which could very well tie his nephew to the bombing. Aurelio had no intentions from backing off.

"Yes, we're going to sit here for as long as we need to. I called a friend at the attorney general's office to get me a search warrant. We should be able to make entry shortly. Until then, sit tight and keep your eyes open for anything and keep radio chatter to a minimum. I'll let you know when we're ready to go."

"Copy that boss."

Aurelio's senses were on heightened alert, looking for anything that seemed out of place. He rolled down his window to get some fresh air, but only got a small blast of the morning heat. As he sank back into his seat, a car turned a corner at the top of the hill and started driving in his direction.

The vehicle was amazing, something only high rollers or people with enough money to blow would purchase. A high-gloss cherry red Aston Martin DBS Volante. For certain, it didn't belong in this neighborhood. The vehicle stopped about halfway down the hill, precisely in the middle of the road. Aurelio's eyes now locked on to his target. Aurelio adjusted his binoculars, trying to gain a better look at the driver, but unfortunately the windows had an extremely dark tint.

"Boss, you seeing this?" a voice whispered over the radio.

"Yeah, I see it. He must have made us, though; he just stopped in the middle of the road."

"Do you want us to move in?"

"No, don't do anything. We don't have any reason to stop him, and I don't want to blow our cover."

Little did Aurelio realize that his mystery drive was his prime suspect, Diego.

Aurelio sat glued to his seat staring, gripping his binoculars tightly causing his fingers to lose circulation. Every fiber in his body screamed at him to close in on that vehicle. However, exercising restraint and using every bit of self-control to not give the order was the smart play here.

He had no doubt that whoever occupied that car, at a minimum, had to be connected to the chop shop, but he couldn't risk blowing his entire operation. He watched as the driver put the vehicle in reverse and suddenly drove backward up the hill. When the car reached the top, it spun the car around and drove out of sight.

"Damn!" Aurelio said.

Then his phone rang. He lowered his binoculars, placing them on the passenger seat. He reached inside his vest, pulling his phone out. "Yeah, this is Aurelio."

"Lieutenant, this is Assistant District Attorney Isabel Cruz. Judge Delgado just signed your search warrant, and you have full authority to go in. I'm on my way to bring it to you."

"Thank you, I appreciate it, Isabel. I'll see you in a few." He ended the call and picked up his police radio.

"Attention all teams, we have a green light to breach, I repeat, we have a green light to breach."

#

Diego might have been sloppy, but he could spot a police stakeout from a mile away and realized it almost instantly. Unmarked police cars had a specific look and feel to them, plus their semi-dark, tinted windows certainly gave them away. As he sat pondering what to do, he realized his best option was to turn around and get the hell away.

He had made a lot of mistakes leading up to this moment but driving right up to the chop shop and walking in with Aurelio and the police sitting on top of him would not be one of them. Diego drove a few miles, continually checking his rearview mirror, trying to asses if he had been tailed by the police.

Hopefully with a small amount of luck, they hadn't spotted him. Diego pulled off on the side of the road to call Ignacio and inform him of the shitty news. After a few rings, Ignacio answered,

"Hey, what's going on? Did you get the van already?"

Already knowing that Diego could not have gotten to the van and disposed of it so quickly. Something wasn't right.

"Hey man, there's a complication. A big one. The shop is crawling with police. Well, I mean, they're camped out all over the place." Diego's voice sounded rushed and panicked.

"I saw your uncle, too. He was parked down the street, in an alley, trying to be inconspicuous. I didn't dare get too close, or they would have seen me. What do you want me to do?"

Diego having no clue he had in fact been spotted, just not identified. Ignacio contemplated for a second, biting his lower lip as he considered the next step. This certainly was a significant blow to his plan, but he had no time to stop and bitch about it, he had to think quickly.

"Meet me at Location One. I think I know how to get my uncle and the police out of there. Get over to Location One."

Location One was a massive warehouse hidden deep in the jungle that had taken his father years to build. Remarkably concealed and remote; the police and the Mexican government could never infiltrate the incredible structure. It was an impenetrable fortress with the dense jungle providing full coverage.

Very few people had to access, the primary intent of location one served as a distribution hub for Vicente's cocaine, marijuana, and weapons shipments, with its secondary use for business meetings or to hold negotiations. This time, however, Ignacio would use it for something dark, evil, and far more demented. He decided this would be the location where he would torture and kill Diego.

"Diego, did you hear me? Meet me at Location One."

"Yeah, I heard you. Why there, though?" Diego asked.

"My father has a plan to throw the cops off track and wants us all to gather in a safe location. Since Aurelio's already been at the compound, he wants to move out there until he's back on his feet. And since it's not that much farther from the compound anyway, those are his wishes."

"What about the van? We're just going to leave it at the shop?"

"You let me worry about that. Like I said, my father has a plan. You just get your ass to Location One as fast as you can. I'll meet you there."

"Okay, I'm on my way."

Ignacio was thirty minutes away, which gave him an advantage with proximity and time. He figured it would take Diego at least sixty minutes to arrive, allowing him more than enough time to set up an ambush. Ignacio tossed his phone on the passenger seat, and in typical Ignacio fashion, revved his engine, rattling the parking area. He slammed the clutch down to the floor, pulled back on the gear shift, and took off like a lightning bolt as he headed to Location One.

#

Aurelio joined six other police cars, swarming the front end of the chop shop, stopping directly in front of the large garage door. Police sirens and flashing lights filled the early morning air. Men wearing black tactical gear, face masks, and helmets flooded out of each vehicle brandishing an array of assault weapons.

With red laser sights firmly affixed to the bottom of each weapon, the streets quickly became flooded with, Heckler & Koch MP7s, UZI submachine guns, Colt M4 assault rifles, Benelli M3 20-gauge shotguns, along with the classic Remington Model 870 16-gauge shotgun. Each officer focused on taking down and killing anyone that was perceived to be a threat.

The first officer breached the front door positioned next to the garage door, blasting a large battering ram near the handle. The door went flying off its hinges. He quickly jumped out of the way, allowing the other officers to enter, all screaming "Policia! Policia!" As the men flooded in and swept through the building, it became soon apparent that no one occupied the building.

Aurelio, the last man through the door, entered the dark, semi-lit room with his flashlight on and his weapon drawn, finger on the trigger. The chop shop was enormous, big enough to easily fit fifteen to twenty cars at a time. It smelled like a chop shop, the familiar odors of motor oil, and grease filled the building. As his men did a sweep, shouting "clear!"

Aurelio noticed a red button on the wall to his right marked "open" and pressed it. The large garage door rolled its way up the track, allowing the sunlight to illuminate the entire place. Aurelio paused for a moment, then put his weapon back in the holster on his leg.

When he received the final all-clear from his men, Aurelio strolled around to the back of the shop to gain a better perspective. That's when he noticed his prize instantly, covered by a large white drop cloth. There was no mistaking what he was looking at. It was his van!

Walking up behind it, he pulled up on the cloth just enough to expose the bumper and license plate. G-F-H-2-9-8-7. He hit the jackpot and now had it in his possession.

"I want this entire area secure," he yelled out.

"This is a secondary crime scene, not a single soul gains access to this building without my direct permission."

He grabbed the rest of the large white cover and pulled it off the van. He dropped the cloth on the floor and walked around the van. As he made his way to the back, a woman's voice called out to him.

"Good morning, Lieutenant. No rest for the wicked?"

He turned and saw Isabel Cruz walking toward him with his warrant.

"No, there never is."

Aurelio opened the warrant and saw that it had been signed by the judge, and everything looked okay to him.

He closed it back up, placing it inside his vest. Isabel starred at the back of the van for a moment.

"So, this is what you've been chasing down?" She didn't sound impressed with his findings.

"Yep, this is it. This is the key to everything."

Isabel paused for a moment.

"I should let you know there are already rumblings down at my office that this may have been an inside job, meaning, within your family. Possibly targeted at the Junta Directiva."

Aurelio hesitated before answering, not wanting to look surprised that rumors had already started to circulate. "C'mon, Isabel, even though we are on the same side, I have to preserve the integrity of the investigation until I write my report."

She smirked at Aurelio, finding his response laughable.

"You're going to make a brilliant politician someday if you decide to step away from law enforcement," she smiled at him.

"I have to get back to my office. I have a meeting with the mayor. Anything you want me to share with him?"

"Just tell him he will have a briefing from me later today."

Isabel turned around and left. As he stood there alone, he felt a little unsettled, knowing that word had already leaked about the Board being present at Vicente's party. Between Ignacio and Vicente, they had half of the police force on their payrolls, so much would not remain a well-guarded secret.

However, this was a massive win for him. He had the van in his possession. All he needed to do was find one fingerprint. One shred of physical evidence linking Ignacio to the van, and he was going to bury him under a jail. It was now time to start processing the crime scene.

Chapter 11: Acts of atrocity

Location one was a massive facility hidden in the middle of the dense, hot Mexican jungle, it easily consumed four football fields. It housed transport airplanes, tons of cocaine shipments neatly wrapped on wooden pallets, custom cars, weapons, and a host of illegal substances. The interior on full display over embellished entirely in white: white floors, white walls, white ceiling, white stairs, everything white.

An impressive fortress, manufactured with reinforced steel columns covered in elaborate aluminum sheets. The entire structure equipped with anti-tracking and minor cloaking capabilities. Everything topped off by a state-of-the-art ventilation system that kept the workers cool, the product dry, and allowed air to flow freely throughout the warehouse.

Heavily armed guards carrying assault weapons patrolled the entire perimeter of the facility, perched high above on catwalks, keeping a close eye on the workers. The outside of the warehouse was just as impressive. Covered from top to bottom with jungle and forest foliage, it made the perfect hidden stronghold.

So many things made this facility unique and majestic. Most notably, it sat perched on a mountainside overlooking a breathtaking waterfall that crashed hundreds of feet to the bottom on jagged rocks. The waterfall created marvelous mists of water floating back up high into the sky. Vicente had his men construct an elaborate tunnel system running throughout the mountain, providing him with quick escape routes if he ever needed them.

Vicente would only allow people two ways to access this location. First, any worker had to be blindfolded when they were picked up from an undisclosed location. At that time, they would be transported by bus for about an hour across narrow desert roads. After being dropped off they would be picked up and escorted by one armed guard through the jungle, eventually reaching the front gate of the heavily guarded by De Los Santos' fortress. Then and only then could they remove their masks.

The second way to access Location one happened by airplane. Before taking off or approaching, any transport or private airplane better have pre-authorization from the security tower. Otherwise, Vicente's standing orders were to shoot anything down. No questions asked. Any government airplanes or drones flying overhead too high up would see nothing but a jungle.

The warehouse structure was entirely concealed. Location one was the symbol that represented the first established meeting with the Junta Directiva after Vicente won the war against each of them. He established his power and assigned them their respective territories and brought peace among them.

With a hefty price tag of fifty million dollars, Vicente thought of it as an investment. To be used as a neutral location for meetings, business matters, and hosting a client or two. However, he committed no acts of violence there. The warehouse bustled with men working feverishly to load and conceal thousands of pounds of drugs into trucks and airplanes.

Ignacio stood in the middle of the warehouse, staring at the surrounding activity. Men walked past him, continuing their activities without anyone paying any attention to him. He kept looking at his watch. Ignacio was nervous, anxious, wanting to get this over with. He had murdered people before, too many to keep count at this point, but this would be different. Ignacio would murder his best friend.

It was almost 9 o'clock when his phone rang, seeing Diego's name he answered.

"Where are you?"

"I'm here, walking down the hallway now. Where are you?"

"I am near the hangar, meet me down near the entrance."

And with that, Ignacio hung up the phone. Ignacio swiftly walked over to the area that overlooked the landing strip at all transport planes coming and going. As he reached the area, he moved a double stack of barrels. Rolling them on their outer circular edge, positioning them to provide him with cover so Diego wouldn't see him when he walked in.

Ignacio tucked himself behind the barrels, placing his back against the wall, peering through a sliver of space between them. Diego entered the hangar and began looking around for Ignacio. He reached into his pocket, digging out his cell phone attempting to call him. With Diego's back to the barrels, Ignacio crept out of the shadows.

Holding his gun by the barrel, he snuck up behind Diego, violently cracking the back of his skull, smashing him with the butt of the gun. Before he realized what even had hit him, Diego dropped to the floor unconscious. He was now at the complete mercy of El Diablo. The lights faded in and out of focus.

The room appeared to be spinning. Diego felt like he was floating. The air in the room was stifling, his face felt warm and wet. Blood streamed down his face. His entire body hurt. As he slowly gained consciousness, he found himself suspended in the air by his arms. His feet barely touching the floor. As he attempted to move, the sounds from the chains ground against each other, making a loud clanking sound.

"What the fuck!"

Diego cried out, sounding terrified. He attempted to pull himself up, only to lose his grip and slip back down, forcing the chains to exert more torque and pain on his shoulders and arms. A single light hung from the ceiling, not allowing much view of the room.

La Familia: Loose Ends

Positioned next to the door saw a metal stand with a silver tray with a cloth covering it. Diego used every ounce of energy he could muster to scream for help.

"HELP! HELP! SOMEONE! ANYONE!"

But there would be no answer. After struggling once more to free himself, he stopped. His shoulders now in too much pain. Unexpectedly, Ignacio's voice appeared from behind him, sending his heart rate into a panic-stricken mode.

"You know I didn't want it to be like this," Ignacio said.

"I did not want it to end this way. You were supposed to be by my side when I ruled. Everything was supposed to work out accordingly. My father would be dead, and I would take his place. But you had to fuck everything up."

Ignacio emerged from the corner of the room. He walked around in front of Diego, stopping to lean against the wall. Diego stared at him. He realized everything his so-called best friend had said to him had been a ploy, a trap to get him here, and now he would use him as a scapegoat for the entire thing.

Ignacio continued.

"If you had just followed simple instructions and not been so sloppy, we wouldn't be here. I mean fuck, how the hell did you screw things up so badly? An unstable, unpredictable bomb. Getting caught on video with the van driver. And leaving the van in my chop shop? Man, you were really begging me to kill you."

Ignacio now flashing that devilish smirk on his face that he had displayed so many times before. He took a step forward, pulling the cloth off the silver tray. A visceral fear overtook Diego's body. The tray consumed with weapons of torture. Ignacio stood in front of the tray contemplating which device to use first.

He savored moments like this, eliciting fear and torment in other people. He gazed down at the collection of knives, ice picks, hammers, and small power saws tapping his finger on the steel metal tray.

"Which one to use, which one to use."

He finally decided on a dirty-looking piece of metal known as the mouth opener. It was a simple and effective tool that dentists used to keep their patients' jaws open during a procedure. It was spring-loaded, so when inserted, it would stay in place. Ignacio moved toward Diego, looking him in the eye.

In an act of defiance, Diego spits in Ignacio's face, the ultimate sign of disrespect. Ignacio didn't flinch. He closed his eyes, reached in his back pocket, pulled out a handkerchief, and wiped his face. Ignacio began to unbutton his shirt, removing it then throwing it to the side of the room. Now Ignacio revealed his black ribbed tank top underneath.

He ripped Diego's shirt open, causing the buttons to go flying in several directions. As each button landed on the concrete, it sounded like small pebbles. With Diego's chest now exposed, Ignacio went to work, punching him repeatedly in his stomach and ribs, like a heavy bag in the gym.

Repeatedly, Ignacio landed right and left hooks. Ignacio knew how to throw horribly painful punches, staying tight like a spring coil, each blow made a massive thud. After five minutes of the punishing boxing lesson, Ignacio moved behind Diego, landing several more thunderous shots to his kidneys.

Diego grunted in excruciating pain with every blow, suspended there helplessly. He could feel his ribs contracting and expanding. Eventually, he heard his ribs pop as they broke. Ignacio walked back around to stand in front of Diego.

Now hot, sweaty and slightly tired, Ignacio mustered up enough energy to throw a front forward kick, landing directly in Diego's stomach. It sent his body back as if he were a slab of meat on a hook.

La Familia: Loose Ends

Diego couldn't breathe, gasping for air. His internal organs felt as if they would explode. Ignacio kicked him with such incredible force that the sole of his shoe left an imprint on Diego's stomach. After a few seconds of spinning around on the chains and attempting to gain even a slight chance at air, Diego started to cough. Ignacio giving him no chance to rest grabbed his hair, whipping his head back and began to choke him.

Diego grunted and gurgled, flailing his body around, hopelessly attempting to free himself. Ignacio squeezed tightly, enough to weaken him even more. After what seemed like an eternity, Ignacio released his grip, allowing Diego's head to fall forward limp. Diego now too exhausted and defeated to put up any sort of struggle. Ignacio lifted Diego's head.

As his eyes rolled into the back of his head, Ignacio spits in his face. Afterwards, he walked back over to the small tray and retrieved the mouth opener. He pulled Diego's head back and forced the opener into his mouth.

Grabbing another instrument off the metal tray, Ignacio pulled his head back again.

"Don't worry. I'm not going to kill you. I'll leave that for my father to do."

He then patted him on the top of his head like a dog.

"But will I have to incapacitate you, so you can't tell him anything."

With tremendous force he snapped Diego's head up, reaching inside his mouth, grabbing his tongue. Diego tried to shake his head free from Ignacio's grip.

"Hey . . . hey . . . hey, keep the fuck still."

Ignacio grumbled. Standing there with Diego's tongue in hand, he grabbed a pair of surgical scissors. Ignacio threw Diego a menacing look and began to cut off his tongue. He had to squeeze tightly on the scissors to get them to cut through the thick, tough muscle.

Diego, now in agony, screamed blood-curdling cries as blood poured out of his mouth. Each cut, each slice, sounded like a rough piece of leather being cut. Finally, Ignacio had managed to cut out a sizeable portion of Diego's tongue and threw it on the floor.

Ignacio stepped back, now covered in the blood of his former friend. Diego had known Ignacio to be a ruthless bastard but could have never imagined that one day he would be on the receiving end of his brutality. He hung there, crying, watching the blood from his mouth fall to the floor.

He hoped he'd be lucky enough to bleed out and die soon. In the back of his mind, though, he knew he would not be that lucky. The De Los Santos family was known for being merciless. Ignacio stood there, wiping his hands with a towel. He walked over to a chair and retrieved his shirt.

"You know, for what it's worth, this isn't personal. I don't hate you. I meant what I said. I wanted you by my side while I sat on the throne. But I guess it just wasn't meant to be. Now, I'll have to find a different way. You, unfortunately, are the collateral damage of it all. Everyone will believe me when I tell them you planned it, put it together, and executed it without me knowing. Ok, so now you hang tight."

Ignacio chuckled.

"No pun intended. I'm going to go and inform my family about how you tried to get the van out of the chop shop to clean up your mess, and when I tracked you down here and confronted you, you attacked me and tried to kill me. That's why I had to incapacitate you."

Ignacio finished buttoning his shirt, opened the door, and turned off the light. He left Diego hanging there in the dark while he headed back to the compound to talk with his father.

La Familia: Loose Ends

#

Now that Vicente was awake and moving around, he wanted to piece together what happened that day, or at least what he still remembered.

"I want to go upstairs and be with Lucita," he said to Gabriella as he sat on the edge of the gurney. Santino walked over to his father and placed his arm around his waist as Gabriella did the same thing on the other side of him.

"No, your mother can do it."

Santino decided not to argue with his father.

"Yes, father, I will meet you upstairs."

He turned and walked out of the room. Gabriella was attempting to lift Vicente up when he slumped back against the table.

"I don't want to go upstairs. I said that to get Santino to leave the room. We need to talk about this Diego situation."

Gabriella helped to ease Vicente back on the gurney. She then turned to face him. They stared at each other for a moment but said nothing. Gabriella was the first to speak.

"It doesn't make any sense," she said.

"Why would Diego want to kill all of us? And how could he think he would be able to run our business on his own?"

Gabriella not understanding the holes with Ignacio's story.

Vicente responded.

"Really, you don't think the same man that has killed countless people for me is not capable of trying to kill us? This is the same man, might I remind you, that helped our son to completely wipe out and murder entire families that opposed us. He is heartless, and if Ignacio says he has evidence, then I believe him. What else happened yesterday?"

Gabriella looked down at the floor, not sure what to say or think. All she understood for certain was that her family had been attacked, and justice needed to be served.

"I don't know. None of this makes sense to me. We treat Diego well, we always have. What made him turn on us?"

"What makes anyone do what they do or act the way they do?" Vicente said.

"Money, power, respect, everyone thinks they can do your job better than you. When I get my hands on him, he is going to suffer. That I can assure you! There aren't many places that the dog can hide. He has no friends or allies. I am sure by now, word has gotten out, and everyone is looking for him. With him attacking not just me but the entire Junta Directiva, all of Mexico will be looking for him!"

Vicente hobbled up to one leg, still grimacing in pain. As he spun around to place both hands on the table, Gabriella's phone rang. She looked down at the number.

"It's your brother. I'm going to take this."

Vicente said nothing, still looking off into the distance.

"Yes, Aurelio. What can I do for you?"

"I need to speak with you. There is something I need to tell you, it's urgent."

"I'm going to put you on speaker. Vicente is awake." Gabriella replied as pressed a button on her phone.

"Okay, go ahead."

"Hello, Vicente. I won't bother asking how you feel. And I'm sure by now you're already aware I was there. I saw the injuries you suffered. I'm certain you're in a great deal of pain. I will keep this short, but you both need to know this. I have confirmation on one of the dead children."

Gabriella held her breath as she stared at the phone. Vicente continued to stare off into the distance. Neither of them said anything. Neither of them ready for what Aurelio was about to tell them.

"Alejandra Rivera."

A deafening silence fell in the room.

Vicente whipped around; his eyes grew wide. Instantaneously he comprehended the full gravity of the moment. Gabriella placed her hand over her mouth in an attempt to stifle a cry and hold back her scream. Tears streamed down her face. She felt sick. Her face turned hot, she thought she might pass out. Vicente snatched the phone from Gabriella.

"How the hell . . . are you certain? Who confirmed this information for you?" Vicente hollered.

"I got a call from the medical examiner. He's one-hundred percent positive. Dental and medical records have confirmed it's her." Aurelio replied.

Vicente paused once again, re-examining the ramifications of what this would mean. Felix Rivera would be out for blood.

"What about Felix? Did he survive? Have you notified him?" Vicente's voice sounded shaky, uneven. Gabriella could see he was in distress.

"I have not received word whether or not he survived the blast, I will assume at this point he is still very much alive. However, I am not ready to release that news to the family. I don't want the news media to get a hold of this until I am ready. Listen, I have to go. I just thought you needed to know first."

With that, Aurelio ended the call. Vicente dropped his head in utter disbelief. He and Gabriella said nothing to each other. They were completely numb; both in mourning as if they had just lost a child. Vicente did not have many rules when it came to winning and war, but he had no room for killing children.

Alejandra's death was a game-changer. If Felix survived the explosion, there would be an all-out war.

"What are we going to do?" Gabriella asked.

"We are going to protect our family at any cost." Vicente clenched his fist, slamming it down on the table.

"When I get my hands on that fucking little shit, Diego, I will make him suffer. And where the hell is Ignacio? He's been gone forever. Get him on the phone."

Vicente tossed the phone back at Gabriella. It hit her in her midsection, causing her to flinch. She fumbled to catch it before it fell to the floor. As she dialed his number, he came slamming through the metal doors.

"You need to come with me right now!" Ignacio yelled.

"Slow down, what is it?" Vicente demanded.

"I will explain on the way. I need you to come with me right now!"

"What the hell do I look like to you? One of your stupid little friends? What the fuck is going on?"

"I have Diego."

Before Vicente had time to respond, Gabriella blurted out. "What do you mean you have him?"

"When I left here, I started tracking the GPS in his car. It brought me over to the chop shop. I caught up with him, and witnessed him starting to approach the shop, but backed off. The place was crawling with police. I followed called him, telling him that I had spoken with you and you wanted everyone over at Location One."

Ignacio turned to his father.

"I'm sorry for using your name for a lie, but I knew he would not disobey an order from you. I arrived at Location One first and waited for him. When he got here, he was moody, on edge, distracted, almost combative.

La Familia: Loose Ends

I asked him what the hell was going on, but he wouldn't say anything, he started texting on his phone. He was pissing me off with his dismissive attitude, so I brought him back into the hangar section. I flat out confronted him about everything. He freaked out and attacked me. We started fighting right there. I was able to knock him out and disable him. I started to interrogate him, but he wouldn't tell me anything, so I told him I was coming to get you, and you would get it out of him."

Vicente had mixed feelings about what Ignacio had just told him. He never used Location One for violence before, so this didn't sit well with him. However, he had the treasonous dog ready to be slaughtered.

"Take me to him," Vicente said.

He began pulling the heart monitor leads off his chest. Gabriella stepped over to him and looked into his eyes. She brought her hands up to his face, cracking a slight smile.

"I love you, my dear." She paused for a moment.

"Now go make him suffer for what he's done against our family." She leaned in, giving him a hug and a kiss on his cheek. She stepped to the side as Ignacio handed him his clothes.

After almost twenty-four hours of being incapacitated, Vicente was now about to exact revenge on the animal who committed violence against his family. He walked out of the room following Ignacio, down the hall, and up the stairs, out to the parking area. He held up his hands to shield his eyes from the sun.

His limp slowed him down a bit, but his ribs bothered him even more. Vicente looked around his compound to see his men posted everywhere all starting at him. Ignacio whistled, then screamed to one of them.

"Go and get the Hummer!"

His man nodded, running off behind one of the buildings. Vicente always appreciated his life and remembered what he had to go through to gain his power. He closed his eyes attempting to taking in a deep breath, allowing the hot air to blow against him. Vicente allowed all of his senses to experience the moment, feeling a little more appreciative to be alive.

Ignacio's man finally pulled up in an impressive, custom-made, armored-reinforced yellow H1 Alpha Hummer. The mighty diesel engine rumbled loudly as he pulled up right next to Ignacio. The guard exited the vehicle, rushing around to open the door for Vicente.

The soldier said nothing as he looked at him. It was evident that he was still in terrible shape. Vicente, in return, said nothing to the guard as he slowly climbed his way into the massive vehicle. The guard closed the door behind him and stepped back. Ignacio and Vicente were now on their way to confront Diego. Little did Vicente realize that his attacker, his would-be killer, was sitting right next to him, and he was about to kill an innocent man.

#

As Aurelio processed the chop shop, he kept wondering if he had made the right decision letting that mysterious vehicle drive off earlier. Who was bold enough to come and collect the van? It was obviously a crucial piece in this puzzle. As he leaned against a wall, sipping his coffee, watching his technicians scour the van for evidence, his phone rang. He pulled it out, seeing it was the chief medical examiners number appear.

"Hello, this is Aurelio."

The medical examiner sounded frazzled, scared, and definitely out of breath.

"Lieutenant, I had no way of stopping him; he and his men barged right in. He knows! He knows!"

Aurelio attempted to calm him down so he could understand what he was saying.

"Whoa, calm down, take a breath. Who knows?"

"Felix Rivera knows his daughter Alejandra is dead. He came down here after they released him from the hospital. His men broke down the front door and gave one of my employees a beating. Felix threatened to kill me if I got in his way. He made me take him to his daughter's body. When he saw her burned remains, he absolutely lost it. Felix started screaming how his only daughter was dead, and blood would be paid back by the gallons."

The medical examiner paused to catch his breath.

"He grabbed me and pinned me to the wall and threatened to cut off my head if I didn't give him whatever information I had. I told him very little, that fifteen people had died in the blast, and most of them were children. He questioned me about Vicente and Lucita. I told him they had both survived, but Vicente was in bad shape. His eyes were blood-shot red. I could feel the heat emanating from his body—his rage, his hate—this was something completely different."

Aurelio pushed himself off the wall and threw his cup of coffee down.

"Okay. It's okay. I'll send some of my men over to stand guard.

They won't let anyone else in."

He hung up the phone.

"Fuck!"

Now that Felix Rivera knew his daughter was dead, this changed everything. He could feel the pressure swelling in his head. He had to find the person responsible for this attack before Felix did, or an all-out war would ensue. Just as he picked up his phone to make another call, one of his technicians called his name.

"Lieutenant, I think I have something!"

As Aurelio walked over, the technician held up a piece of thin, transparent plastic with two dark fingerprints in the middle of it.

"I have two different fingerprints that I lifted from the inside of the van. They're solid prints, so if they're in the database, I can find your guy."

Aurelio's heart started beating fast.

"I want you to go right now and run those prints. You don't report back to anyone else but me, do you understand?"

"Yes, sir." The technician nodded and started walking away.

"Get the fuck moving . . . RUN!" Aurelio hollered.

Without looking back, the young technician darted off. Aurelio prayed that this was the break he needed to catch who was responsible. He picked up his phone and called Gabriella. The phone rang and rang and rang. Aurelio hung up quickly, redialing her number, but there was no response.

He didn't know if she was ignoring him or if Vicente had told her not to speak to him anymore. Regardless, he had to get word to her that Felix Rivera had was aware of his daughter's death and to keep an eye out. Aurelio attempted called Gabriella back one last time and left a voice-mail message.

"Gabriella, you know who this is. Felix Rivera just found out that Alejandra is dead. You all need to be careful. Call me when you get this."

#

As the Hummer drove along the rough and uneven jungle road, each bump jarred Vicente's broken ribs. He grimaced in pain as he tried to steady himself.

"Slow down, you idiot!" he screamed at Ignacio.

The drive also gave him time to question Ignacio about Diego.

"So, tell me something. How was your number two man, the person who reports directly to you, able to pull all off this massive attack without you knowing? I mean, are you really trying to convince your mother and me that you had no knowledge about this? What does that say about your leadership and your ability to watch over your men?"

Ignacio hated his father, especially in times like this, when he questioned everything he did and belittled him. He showed him no sign of respect as a man or a leader. He realized that he had to keep his cool though, as this was already a hostile situation, and if he wanted to make this work, he needed to be humble and play along.

"I get why you're questioning everything father; I do. Yeah, I look like an asshole right now. My number two man orchestrated all of this behind my back. I have no defense for that. He tried to kill you, Mamá, Lucita, and the board. If you want to hold me accountable for this, I'll accept my punishment. I need you to know though, that the moment I suspected something and started tracking Diego, I came right back to report it to Mamá."

Vicente not satisfied with his son's shallow answer, cut to the chase.

"Did you have anything to do with this attack on us?" Vicente hoped the question would startle Ignacio, catch him off guard. Ignacio snapped his head over at his father.

"Are you kidding me? How could you ask me something like that? How could I ever hurt you, or Mamá, or Lucita?

And plotting to assassinate the entire board of directors? That would be suicide! I had absolutely nothing to do with this."

Vicente didn't trust many people. In fact, he trusted no one. He had to keep those who were closest to him on a short leash. It was how he operated.

"I ask because I raised you. I know how you think. You are a mirror image of me. If I was looking to rise to power, I would have done the same thing. That's why I had to ask. For now, I believe you, Ignacio. I believe you had nothing to do with this."

Ignacio sat looking relaxed as he breathed a small sigh of relief on the inside, as they arrived at the front gates of Location One. As they drove up to the enormous steel gates, a guard approached their vehicle with his weapon ready. Just as he walked up to the driver's side door, the dark-tinted window rolled down, exposing both Ignacio and Vicente.

The guard wasted no time walking back to the gate entering the access code. The massive hydraulic gates powered opened allowing Ignacio to drive down into a very short tunnel, which led them to the heart of Location One. They drove past all the men hard at work loading trucks and airplanes for their next shipments.

Ignacio pulled into the hangar area, parking the massive Humvee—right next to the soon to be infamous room. Ignacio exited the vehicle first, then walked around to the passenger side to open the door for his father. Vicente had already opened his door carefully climbing his way out.

By now Vicente's adrenaline was kicking in, providing him with a much-needed break from the pain. The animal savagery he was experiencing put him in a different mindset where the pain had no place.

Ignacio led the way to the room where he had left Diego.

As he reached for the doorknob, Vicente interrupted him.

"Wait, I want to be the first face he sees when we walk in." Ignacio stopped and stepped to the side. Vicente grabbed the doorknob, turning it slowly, pushing the door open. The light from the hangar fell on Diego's body, not yet fully exposing the damage he had suffered at the hands of Ignacio.

Vicente turned on the light. He quickly realized that when Ignacio had said he disabled Diego, he meant he had tortured the hell out of him. Diego's body flinched, causing him to spin slightly from the chains he was suspended from. Vicente walked into the room but said nothing. He looked at the carnage and mess that hung before him. Ignacio followed right behind him and closed the door.

Vicente circled Diego like a lion stalking its kill. He walked around him, continuously. Finally stopping in front of Diego, grabbing him by his hair, lifting his head up. Diego's eyes rolled to the back of his head. He was half awake, half unconscious. Vicente glared at him. No longer contain himself and the rage building up inside him.

"Do you see what you have done? Do you see what you have done to my family and me? Look at me. I look weak and pathetic. You almost killed my wife and my little daughter at her birthday party! Like a coward! And you had the balls to attack Junta Directiva? Are you stupid or something? I treated you good. Like you were my own son. I treated you like family, and this is how you repay me, you filthy coward?"

Vicente stepped back and spit on Diego, while slapping him across the top of his head.

"And not to mention how you betrayed your own friend, my son you grew up with, ate meals with, slept in the same bed with."

"YOU FILTHY FUCKING PIECE OF SHIT!"

Ignacio muttered in the background. Up to this point, he had said nothing. He stood behind his father; happy his plan was working. Compelled to look and play the part, Ignacio stood next to his father staring at Diego.

"I trusted you. You were like my brother. I would have given anything to you. How could you fucking betray me? Betray us like this? You're nothing to me now. There is a special place in hell for people like you!"

With that last remark, deep down inside Ignacio realized was speaking of himself. Still, he would leave nothing to chance and leave no room for doubt in his father's mind and give the performance of a lifetime. Vicente stepped back a few feet wanting to hit Diego so badly, but he knew he wasn't steady enough on his feet yet.

Vicente turned around and started eyeballing the small metal tray Ignacio had set up. He limped over to the tray grabbing an ice pick with an old wooden handle. Turning back around, he walked over to Diego and placed the tip of the ice pick in his left armpit. Slowly pushed the long rusty ice pick into Diego's body, twisting the sharp object.

Diego let out a cry, still with the mouth opener in place. Once Vicente had the ice pick deep into Diego's armpit, he used all of his strength to slam on the end of the wooden handle with his other hand, shoving it in as far as it would go. Diego once again screamed in excruciating pain. Vicente pulled the ice pick out slowly handing it to Ignacio.

Vicente struggled as he unbuckled Diego's pants, Diego attempting to twist, shake and turn to avoid him, but it was useless. Vicente pulled Diego's pants down, exposing his legs, once again grabbing the ice pick from Ignacio. He began to sadistically scrape the sharp metal tip up and down Diego's leg eventually plunging the ice pick into Diego's leg, searching for the bone.

When he could finally sense the tip of the ice pick touching bone, Vicente started making slow, repeated stabbing motions while simultaneously twisting the ice pick. A tactic known as "bone tickling."

Diego started spinning too much causing Ignacio to hold him. He stepped behind Diego, grabbing him around his waist, allowing his father to continue jamming the rusty ice pick into his leg. After several minutes, Vicente was ready for something different. Something that would be just as unbearable, but not kill him.

Vicente wasn't big on elaborate tortures. He always felt he could make a statement with simple ways to hurt people. Every now and then, he would overstate how he had killed, but at the end of the day, he kept it simple. He grabbed a scalpel off the table holding the razor-sharp knife right in front of Diego's face.

"I am going to cut you fifteen times, one for each of the people you killed at my daughter's party."

His voice was dead and calm.

Vicente made a diagonal slice from Diego's shoulder down to his belly.

"That's one."

He then walked behind Diego, stabbing him in his leg, severing his left hamstring. Repeating the same act to Diego's right leg. Diego flopped around like a fish, dangling from the chains screaming. Like a predator, Vicente once again circled Diego. Making small incisions all over his body. Along his rib cage, down his arms, across his face, and along his forehead.

He cut Diego fifteen times, exactly as he said he would do—one for every death at his party. Diego was on the verge of death. His body not able to take much more physical pain. Mentally he was ready to die. He had lost a tremendous amount of blood by now, and it was just a matter of time before his body quit working.

Everything that had been done to him up to this point had lived up to the unfortunate truth about the De Los Santos family and their propensity for violence. Vicente stood glaring at Diego, not yet satisfied with how much pain he had endured. He looked at Ignacio and motioned for him to come next to him. Vicente leaned in and whispered something in his ear. Ignacio left the room, leaving the two of them alone.

Vicente stood there for a moment, then reached over and grabbed a pair of pliers from the table.

"Maybe you cannot hear so good, so I will help you."

Vicente reached up to grabbing Diego's left ear with the pliers. Diego tried to wriggle away but to no avail. Vicente grabbed the top of Diego's ear and started pulling down with a tremendous amount of force. Diego could hear the cartilage in his head begin to pop and crack as Vicente tore off his ear.

Eventually, his flesh could not withstand the pressure being applied and peeled away from Diego's head. Diego screamed, writhing in pain. The sinister expression on Vicente's face was one of pure evil and pleasure. He took a sick enjoyment in knowing that this dog was suffering.

Finally, the ear gave way, causing Vicente to jerk backward. Although he hadn't pulled the entire ear off, he got a large chunk of it. Grasping the chunk of Diego's ear in the pliers, he tossed it to the floor. He watched Diego's body swing around as blood poured from the side of his head. Ignacio walked back into the room, holding a large brown glass jug. It was going to be part of the final act in Vicente's horror show.

#

Aurelio just started to take a bite out of a sandwich he got out of a vending machine. It wasn't much, but anything would do at this point, considering he had not eaten now for almost nineteen hours. His phone rang. Aurelio reached into his pocket to retrieve his cell phone, realizing that it was the police station.

"Yeah, this is Aurelio."

"Lieutenant, this is the technician from the shop. I have a hit on both of those fingerprints."

Aurelio hoped to hear some good news. "Okay, go ahead. What do you have?"

"The first print belongs to Ruben Rodriguez. He goes by the street name Jaguar. He has a lengthy criminal history."

BINGO. Aurelio thought, this was his van driver. The technician continued.

"The second print we lifted belongs to a Diego Sanchez, he too . . ."

"Are you sure? Rerun it." Aurelio blurted.

"I have run it, twice, both of them as a matter of fact. I am one-hundred percent sure that these two fingerprints belong to these two people."

Aurelio couldn't believe it. He had Diego dead to rights beyond a shadow of a doubt. Now he had to get his hands on him.

"You keep this information between the two of us. I'll speak to you later."

Aurelio hung up and immediately called his sergeant, knowing he needed to secure an arrest warrant for both Ruben and Diego. Pressing his speed dial, the phone rang twice when he finally heard Sergeant Ramos pick up. Before he Ramos even say hello or his own name, Aurelio started speaking.

"I need you to issue arrest warrants for Diego Sanchez and Ruben Rodriguez. Both on probable cause of attempted murder and do it now!"

"Yeah sure . . . is that it?"

"Yeah, that's it. Get on it now. I want them both picked up by tonight!"

Little did Aurelio realize there would be no chance of that ever happening. Jaguar was long gone by now, buried alive in an unmarked grave, and Diego was being ruthlessly tortured and facing imminent death. Aurelio realized time was not on his side. He walked over to the crime scene commander.

"I want this entire place processed in one hour. I'm going out in the field. Radio me when you are done."

Aurelio did not want to wait for his men to find Diego or Jaguar. He, too, had to be out there actively looking. Plus, he didn't want to take the chance that one of Vicente's men might get a hold of them first. The henchmen from the Junta Directiva might be after them as well. He started jogging to his police car, anxious to get his search started.

His phone rang. It was Gabriella.

"Hello Gabriella, are you and the family okay?" he asked with a note of concern in his voice.

"Yes, we are fine. I got your message. How did Felix learn of Alejandra's death? I thought you weren't going to tell anyone."

"I wasn't. I would never put you or the family in danger like that. Felix made his way down to the medical examiner's office and demanded to see his daughter's body. He lost it, screaming of revenge and blood. You all need to stay where you are, do you understand me? Don't move!"

Gabriella didn't dare tell Aurelio that Vicente and Ignacio were already gone.

"Yes, I understand. We aren't going anywhere. What about yourself? You are aware your life is now in danger too."

Aurelio appreciated the gesture of concern. It was nice knowing he was not entirely hated by all members of his family.

"I'll be fine. If Felix feels the need to come after me to get revenge against Vicente, he knows where to find me.

Sensing an opening, Aurelio thought he would capitalize on the moment of goodwill.

"Hey, let me ask you. Diego wouldn't happen to still be with you, would he?" The line sat quiet.

Gabriella paused, not sure how she should answer that question. If Aurelio was asking about Diego, there had to be a reason. She knew she had to give him a safe answer.

"No. Diego left about an hour ago. He said he needed to get collections rolling again. I have not spoken with him since."

Aurelio was slightly disappointed with the answer. He was almost hoping that all he needed to do was head back to the compound and pick Diego up, but in his line of work, nothing ever came that easy.

"Why, are you inquiring about him?"

Gabriella asked.

Now it was Aurelio who was uncertain on how to answer her question. He was not about to come right out and tell her he had obtained fingerprints that belonged to the driver of the van. He, too, gave a safe answer that would make sense.

"I just want to do some more follow up with him, nothing too heavy, but he may have some insight about a van that was seen driving up to your house . . . that's all."

Gabriella didn't want to fall too deep into a conversation about Diego.

"I cannot hand him over to you, but when I see him, I will tell him you're looking for him. Fair enough?"

"Fair enough. You take care. Oh, and by the way. How is my niece?"

"She is fine for now. She's with Santino, but I am sure this will haunt her forever."

"I'm sure it will, too. It's not my job to tell you how to be her parent. All I will say is give her extra love and support so she can start to heal and feel safe again. Give her a hug from me, too. I will talk to you later."

"I will, thank you, Aurelio."

When Aurelio reached his car, he couldn't help but notice the already unbearable heat of the day. The sun was out, and there wasn't a single cloud to be found in the sky. The sluggish breeze of the sizzling air had already made the inside of his police car feel like a portable oven. He was hit with a blast of fiery heat as he opened his door. He started the engine and drove away to attempt to track down both Diego and Jaguar. Maybe he would get lucky and find them together.

#

Diego's body slowly spun around like a slab of meat on a hook waiting to be carved up by a butcher. His entire body had suffered so much unimaginable trauma that his whole central nervous system had begun to shut down. He was fading in and out of consciousness, but a small part his mind was still strong enough to pray to La Virgen de Guadalupe, the Patron Saint of forgiveness for past crimes.

Vicente stood there, relishing the moment, watching Diego hanging there and mumbling incoherently. He held the brown glass jug that Ignacio had brought into the room. After a moment, he placed it on the floor, glancing over at Ignacio.

"Is there anything you wish to say or do to this dog before I put him down?"

Ignacio understood he still had to play the part. He said nothing, as he walked over to Diego. The room was like a steam sauna, especially after all the physical abuse they had laid on Diego.

Ignacio was sweaty. He removed his shirt as he walked behind Diego.

He wrapped his shirt around Diego's neck, grabbing each sleeve, and began to slowly choke him, but not enough to kill him, however. As Diego's head jerked back, Ignacio placed his mouth close to Diego's ear.

"I loved you like you were my own brother; I loved you more than my own brother. There is no forgiveness for someone like you."

Ignacio released his grip on his shirt reaching behind his back, pulling out a six-inch knife. He propelled his arm forward, thrusting the knife deep into Diego's back with surgical precision, severing his spine. Diego's legs went limp, no longer with the ability to feel anything below his waist, he had been completely immobilized.

Vicente looked at Ignacio with a sick, twisted pride. Knowing that his son had the ability to make such bold choices, sacrificing someone close to him in the face of adversity, set him at ease in his demented mind. Vicente still clueless to the fact his son had tried to sacrifice and murder him.

"Run and get one of the hauling trucks ready,"

Vicente said.

"Make sure it has a barrel on it. There won't be much left."

Ignacio looked at his father and nodded. As he walked to the door, he turned to take one last glimpse at Diego. His mind quickly flashed back through a lifetime of memories with Diego. Ignacio remembering them as kids running around playing soccer, smiling and laughing—long before the evils of the underworld had consumed them.

Stealing candy from the corner store, hot-wiring cars, and taking them for joy rides. That was when life had been enjoyable and straightforward. Now all the wonderful memories from childhood had been erased by this betrayal. His betrayal of his dear friend.

However, Ignacio now at the point of no return was willing to live with it to save his own skin. He had helped to murder his best friend. In an attempt to murder his father, he had almost killed his family and the entire Junta Directiva. He was in the fast lane to hell now.

To achieve the power he wanted, Ignacio would have to be okay with sacrificing whoever he needed to. Ignacio exited the room, leaving Vicente all alone with Diego. Although Vicente had exacted the revenge he wanted, he still needed to see Diego suffer one last, final time. He took a pair of rubber gloves off the metal table and pulled them on.

Vicente reached down and picked up the brown glass jug. He pulled out the large cork tossing it to the floor. The smell was overpowering, forcing Vicente to turn his head away. The odor reeked of noxious, rotten eggs and sulfur. Vicente coughed to clear his lungs. Then, holding the jug out to his side to avoid the hideous vapors, he walked up to Diego's now seemingly lifeless body.

He lifted Diego's head up, with the mouth opener still in place. He began pouring the hydrochloric acid down his throat. Diego gagged and screamed. Vicente quickly jumped aside to avoid getting splattered. Not giving Diego any chance to rest, he grabbed his head once again, and continued pouring the acid on his face and chest.

Diego's flesh dissolved as the acid made its way through his body, eating away at his muscles, tendons, ligaments, and joints. His lips were becoming liquefied. Now only able to make horrifying gurgling sounds as he choked on his blood and the acid. His lungs were disintegrating. The smell of Diego's burning, liquefying body, forced Vicente to cover his own mouth and nose.

Satisfied that nothing more needed to be done, he left the room. A few minutes later, Ignacio drove up in a large white pickup truck with a wooden frame around the cargo bed. He got out and walked to the rear of the truck lowering the lift gate.

Ignacio stepped up into the truck and maneuvered a large, red plastic double-walled barrel onto a large dolly, then put it on the lift gate and lowered it. He wheeled the dolly over to the door where his father stood.

"Clean up your mess and get rid of the body,"

Vicente ordered.

"Come to my office when you're done."

Vicente turned and limped away. Ignacio said nothing. He wasn't surprised his father would leave the rest to him, but he still resented it. He forced the door to the room open, swinging it hard enough to slam against the wall. When he opened the door instantly, he was hit with the gut-wrenching smell of burning flesh and rotten eggs.

Ignacio gagged. Dry heaves bent him over at the waist. When he looked up, he saw Diego's half-melted body. In all his years of working for his father, this had to be the worst form of death he had ever witnessed. He wheeled the dolly into the room.

Still overpowered by the smell, Ignacio ran back to retrieve a face mask from the truck, so he wouldn't have to inhale any more of the disgusting stench. Still while at the truck he pulled out from the back seat a heavy rubber apron and rubber gloves placing everything on. Ignacio positioned the barrel and dolly next to Diego's melting body.

He reached into his pocket grabbing keys to the lock on the chain that Diego was handcuffed to. Ignacio realized he had to be careful to avoid getting any of the acid or melted flesh on his body. He used one hand to unlock the handcuffs from the large metal chain and the other to shove Diego's body toward the barrel.

His aim was good—half of it slumped in. Ignacio worked quickly to shove the rest of the body into the barrel. It was nothing but a contorted mess. The upper body was still dissolving and breaking apart, so it wasn't hard to make everything fit.

He reached down and grabbed the lid. He took one last look at his now very dead former friend.

"Rest easy, Hermano."

He whispered, paying one last respect to the innocent tortured soul, he had just sent on to the afterlife. He placed the lid on the barrel clasping the two steel locks and encasing Diego inside his eternal resting place. Ignacio wheeled the dolly back out to the pickup and loaded the barrel onto the cargo bed.

He grabbed two straps to secure it for transport. Once the barrel was secure, he jumped down and raised the lift gate. Confident everything was good to go, he walked back into the hangar and whistled for one of his men to come over.

A short, stocky, muscular-looking promptly ran over. Ignacio stepped up close getting right in his face.

"You need to listen to me very carefully because your life depends on it."

"Yes, boss. Whatever you need," the man replied.

"I want you to go and dispose of this barrel. Take another man with you. Find a remote, inaccessible location far into the heart of the jungle. Dig a deep hole and bury it. If this barrel is ever found, you'll be buried in the next one. Do you understand me?"

The man looked into Ignacio's eyes, trying not to look panic-stricken. Ignacio stretched out his hand and dangled the keys to the truck in front of him.

"Do you understand me?"

Ignacio said again.

The man nodded.

"Yes, Señor De Los Santos."

The man grabbed the keys and headed back into the hangar where he motioned to another man to come with him. The two hurried back to the pickup and took off, Ignacio watching them drive away. His plan had worked, and he was in the clear. With Diego gone now, there would be no more suspicion about the bombing at the family's home. He turned and headed back in to meet his father.

#

As Vicente sat in his spectacular office overlooking the warehouse, he sipped on a rare brand of whiskey. He needed something to take the edge off as his pain had slowly crept back into his body. He turned on the television and immediately saw the news was still reporting about the attack on his family.

The female journalist was reporting live from the gates outside his home as a long line of police cars finally were seen leaving the property. The reporter was speaking as to who would have the courage to commit such a brazen act. Done against the most powerful family in all of Mexico.

Seeing the cops were leaving was a great sign for Vicente. It meant they had concluded their investigation and that he and his family could go back home. Ignacio walked into the room, turning his head to see what his father was watching. Vicente turned up the volume. The reporter's voice grew loud.

"Police have not yet released an official statement as to who is responsible for the attack on the De Los Santos family. To recap, what we know at this point is that fifteen people are confirmed dead, eight of them children. Speculation remains heavy, as the entire Board of Director was attending a birthday party here at the time of the attack. Could this have been an attempt to kill and dismantle the entire board, or was this simply an attempt on one man's life— Vicente De Los Santos? We will continue with our coverage throughout the day and more tonight on Channel Five Action News."

Vicente angrily shook the remote at the television screen.

"Do you see what type of trouble your friend has caused us? This will take forever to clean up!"

Vicente's outburst was interrupted by the ringing of his phone. He threw the remote on the couch that sat underneath the television and hobbled over to his desk. Looking at the caller ID, it came up as a restricted number. Vicente was reluctant to pick it up but had a strange feeling he needed to answer.

With the news of the attack on his family being televised, it could have been any number of his business associates trying to reach him. He had to let them know he was still alive and in charge.

"Hello?"

"Do you know what it is like to lose a child?"

The man's voice, on the other end, sounded callous and void.

"It feels like having your soul ripped out of your body, tormenting agony thrashing at your heart. You are missing a piece of yourself that you can never get back. You no longer have any emotion of love or joy, there is only an abyss of wretchedness, unbearable anguish."

It was Felix Rivera.

"Felix, please, let me assure you I had nothing to do with this attack," Vicente said.

" I . . . "

"Shut your mouth, you filthy fucking liar!"

Felix's voice quickly turned to rage.

"Someone as dark and evil as yourself would love to do something like this to get at me, to deflect any attention from yourself. You knew I was coming there to renegotiate a new agreement about our agreement and territories.

Still, you, the Great Vicente De Los Santos, had to make sure you had the upper hand that you remained the most powerful among us. You had your own daughter's party bombed to make it appear like it was an attack on all of us. But only my sweet little Alejandra suffered. You killed her. Don't you think others will find it strange that none of the De Los Santos family was killed in the explosion?"

Vicente understood Felix's pain, but still would not be disrespected. He wouldn't allow anyone to insinuate that he would hurt his own family.

"Why the hell would I put my own family in danger simply to kill a low life like you! I let you come to my home to celebrate my daughter's birthday. If I wanted you dead, I would do it myself!"

The conversation turned volatile.

"Vicente, there will come a day when you will experience what I am feeling, the loss of a child. Until then, every day moving forward, you are going to have to look over your shoulder and wonder, is today Felix Rivera day?"

And with those last menacing words, Felix hung up the phone. What Vicente had always feared was showing its ugly head. Another war was on the horizon, and this time all bets were off. No one was safe. Most importantly, he knew his entire family was now in grave danger.

Vicente would do anything to protect them. Ignacio stood there, saying nothing. He had overheard everything Felix said. This was the first he had heard about the death of Alejandra Rivera. He was shocked and now realized the gravity of the situation. In his attempt to kill his father and assume power, he had killed an innocent little girl. Not just any girl—the daughter of one of the Junta Directiva. He had started an all-out war.

Feeling compelled to say something, Ignacio walked over to his father as he stood at his desk, he placed his hand on his back.

"Papá, I was unaware that Alejandra had died in the attack. I am sorry for your loss. I know you loved her like your own. Felix is just mourning right now; he cannot see straight. Give it time, he will heal and get over it."

Ignacio should have kept his mouth shut.

Vicente immediately straightened his body, whipping around, slapping his son's hand off his back and getting right into his face. "GET OVER IT? . . . GET OVER IT? . . . YOU JUST DON'T GET OVER THE DEATH OF A CHILD, NOT YOUR ONLY CHILD, YOU IDIOT!"

Vicente was in a full tirade.

"This man is going to want blood. He's going to want revenge, and all of us are in danger because of that son-of-a-bitch Diego!" Ignacio had no words. He knew his father was right. Felix would never get over this, and a war was imminent. Vicente quickly picked up his phone.

"I must call your mother."

Vicente was panicked and worried. As he stood there listening to her phone ring, he could only imagine what Felix was planning for him and his family.

"Come on . . . come on . . . pick up the phone."

Finally, after the fourth ring, Gabriella answered.

"Hello, my love. Are you okay?"

"I'm okay. Are you and Lucita okay? Is Santino still with you?"

Immediately Gabriella heard the panic in his voice.

"Yes, we are all fine. We're all here, what is the matter?"

Vicente was preparing to tell Gabriella about the conversation he had just had with Felix. Meanwhile, Gabriella was preparing to tell Vicente that Aurelio had called to notify her earlier.

"I need you to listen to me," Vicente said with urgency in his voice. "You need to stay there and not move until we return. Felix knows, he just called me, he's threatened all of us. He blames me, claiming I set this whole thing up to kill him over our disagreements."

"Yes, Vicente," Gabriella replied.

La Familia: Loose Ends

"I know about Felix. Aurelio called to tell me and said that Felix found out and that we should be careful, but why would Felix say such a thing? He knew how much we loved her! And why would he think you would put our entire family at risk?"

A sense of relief came over Vicente knowing Gabriella was aware and that they were safe still at the family compound. It would take a small military army to attack them there.

"Have we put that other situation to bed yet?"

Gabriella asked.

She was always careful about what she said over the phone.

"Yes, all debts have been paid, and everyone is sleeping comfortably."

Vicente would never share the gory details with her.

"Ignacio and I will leave here soon. You and I have a lot of family business to attend to when I return. We must get everything back on track. I will see you soon, my love."

"Yes, I will see you soon," Gabriella's tone sounding soft and loving.

Ignacio and Vicente both stood in complete silence, each contemplating the series of events that had just occurred over the last twenty-four hours. It was now going on 2 o'clock in the afternoon. By this time, the day before, tragedy was thirty minutes away from befalling their family.

Vicente sat on the edge of his desk, looking down at the floor, rubbing his chin. He was trying to envision all the moves that were about to transpire. Finally, he broke the silence of the room.

"This will get worse before it gets better," he said, still staring at the floor.

"Felix has to go. I will need to replace him. He controls a sizeable portion of southern Mexico, but for obvious reasons,

I cannot trust him anymore. I'm placing you in charge until I find a suitable replacement."

Ignacio couldn't believe what his father had just said, he was appointing him to the Junta Directiva, and still, he remained calm. After everything that had taken place, he was one step closer to gaining the genuine power he was looking for. Vicente stood up and walked over to Ignacio.

"Let me make myself perfectly clear though. This is only temporary. You're a soldier, not a businessman. You kill first, instead of negotiating, that is not the way to do business. That is not how I have been able to keep the peace for so many years. I have raised you to be ruthless because that is what I have needed on the streets—someone to keep everyone in line. However, you will need to exercise restraint. I don't want you attracting attention. Do you understand?"

Ignacio didn't agree with his father's rationale. His way of keeping people in line was using a big stick and using it often. However, Ignacio wasn't about to talk himself out of this opportunity.

"Yes, father, I will not let you down."

Vicente's phone rang once again. He looked at the caller ID. To his surprise and slight disgust, it was Aurelio.

"What do you want?"

he asked with contempt in his voice.

"It's nice to speak to you too, brother," Aurelio replied.

"I know this is a stupid question, but I have to ask. Have you seen your boy, Diego? I need to speak to him."

Once again, Ignacio could overhear the conversation, and both he and Vicente smiled.

"No, I haven't seen him since he left the compound a while ago," Vicente said, "but I did get a frantic and threatening call from Felix

Rivera a little while ago. He was threatening me and my family and anyone I know. Maybe Diego ran into him?"

What a perfect card for Vicente to play, shift any suspicion to Felix. *Shit*, Aurelio thought to himself that would be a worst-case scenario. He would stand no chance of finding Diego.

"So, Felix called you, huh? Then you must know that he knows Alejandra is dead."

"Yes, I am aware he knows, and we are all in danger too. I will boost my security. We'll be safe for now."

Their exchange was awkward and tight, as it always was with no feeling or emotion. It was almost as if they were two strangers. Aurelio broke the long pause between them.

"You take care, brother," he said peaceably.

Vicente returned the gesture.

"You take care, as well."

The two men hung up the phone. Aurelio was tired, hot, sweaty, and starving. He had eaten nothing of actual substance for almost twenty-four hours. Aurelio decided to call it a day and head back to the police station. There he could shower, get a fresh change of clothes, and finally get some long-awaited food in his stomach.

Aurelio got on the highway headed back into town, hoping he could still pick up Diego or Ruben, a.k.a Jaguar if Felix hadn't gotten to them yet. Vicente was ready to head back to the compound and start a new day. Vicente was excited to hug his daughter, hold his wife, and get into a fresh change of clothes.

He wanted to resume his place at the top of the family empire that he had worked so hard to build. He knew that image was everything, and he needed to show the world that he was still intact, and his family was still in control. Ignacio had pulled off his perfect and chaotic plan of not only framing Diego for the attempt on his father's life but also getting rid of him. For now, he felt confident that any clues that pointed to him had been cleaned up.

Vincent and Ignacio headed down to the warehouse where they had parked the Hummer. They climbed in and made their way back through the jungle, leaving behind the horrors they had committed at Location One that day. Before long, they were on their way to the De Los Santos compound, where Vicente De Los Santos would once again take his place as head of the most ruthless drug cartel in Mexico.

The Del Los Santos family had survived an unprecedented attack that almost tore them apart. Little did any of them realize that the mastermind of the attack was still on the loose and still very much bloodthirsty. And he was living right amongst them.

So many questions were still left unanswered, so many loose ends. Had Ignacio cleaned up all the evidence that would possibly point to him? Would Santino suspect his own brother of being capable of this crime? How long would it take for Aurelio to realize he was chasing his tail and would never find Diego or Jaguar?

Would Lucita ever be okay after what she witnessed that day? When was Felix Rivera going to rear his ugly head? Ignacio would have to wait another day to kill his father and take what he saw as his rightful place. Still, for now, he had created a small opening and was on the Junta Directiva. This would start a new chapter for the entire De Los Santos family.

EXCERPT

la Familia: Innocence Lost

Aurelio lay on the ground, critically wounded. The gunshot to his leg bleeding profusely. His face a bloody mess, his nose broken, cheekbone shattered, both of his eyes close to swollen shut, and his jaw was most likely broken. He tasted the blood in the back of his throat as it flowed down into his stomach.

The raging fire in the building now out of control.

Uncertain how long he had been unconscious, he felt nauseous and disorientated from the fall. His ears were ringing; all he heard was the loud whistling sound in his head. Aurelio attempted to lift himself up only to fall flat, the knife still deeply embedded in his left shoulder.

Able to push himself to his knees, he reached around with his other arm, pulling out the knife, letting out a scream as he tossed it aside. Instantly, he fell right back to the ground exhausted, rolling to his back, coughing as smoke consumed the room. In his mind, he knew this was it.

Aurelio was going to die, and sadly he could hear Lucita's beautiful little voice saying to him, "Please Uncle Aurelio, you're not done yet, you have to get up ... PLEASE!" He turned his head to look at the door realizing he was not too far away from the exit. However, the building now raged with flames, was consumed in smoke, and his exit blocked.

His only chance at living would be to jump through the plate-glass window from the second floor where he landed. With every ounce of energy he could muster, Aurelio rolled over to his side, letting out small painful grunts while taking short deep breaths.

Finally, making it to his feet, he staggered, stumbling to gain his balance. Attempting to stay low enough, breathing any remaining oxygen in the room, he limped over to the window, looking down at the hard-concrete landing that awaited him. Aurelio had almost no energy to toss himself through the window.

With his broken ribs, his body beaten and bruised, this for certain would be the last-ditch effort he needed if he would survive. Aurelio banged his shoulder into the window, when a pile of burning wood began to rustle in the corner of the room. Unaware of the movement, he continued to try and break the glass.

On his fourth attempt, the glass shattered, sending the pieces down below. Thinking once and for all he would be free of this nightmare, Aurelio started to shove his leg through the window. Suddenly, El Fantasma grabbed him by his police vest, tossing him back into the fiery room.

He hit the floor with a loud thud, spinning around as he fell to the ground. The Ghost, also gravely wounded, stood tall, blocking the window now fixated on his arch-nemesis. Aurelio could not believe it, *could this really be happening?* He thought to himself. Unfortunately, it was, El Fantasma was not dead, despite being shot directly in the head.

Clutching the hole in the side of his head, The Ghost released the pressure reaching around to his back pocket, pulling out a large serrated hunting knife. When he removed his hand from his head, an enormous gush of blood shot across the room. For a split second, he stumbled feeling dizzy but quickly gained his composure.

As Aurelio attempted to stand up, his hand brushed against the knife laying on the ground that had been used against him earlier.

Grabbing it, he hobbled to his feet, attempting to defend himself. Once again, standing toe-to-toe with the relentless force known as El Fantasma.

The room now completely consumed in fire seemed like the perfect ending for both men. The journey of hell they both had traveled to get there, eventually fate intertwining their paths on an unstoppable collision course. Both men staring at each other, being baptized by the fire of hell that surrounded them, no more words to be said. The Ghost knew after a lifetime of bloodshed, he had met the one man in the world that could kill him. Now both Aurelio and El Fantasma were equally matched. Both men were ready to die. One to protect his family, the other to protect his reputation.

The End

Follow La Familia
www.thedelossantosfamily.com
Twitter: @Real_La Familia
Instagram: lafamilia_delossantos
Facebook: LaFamilia_De Los Santos

Corey Cepeda

About the author

Born on May 1st, 1974 in Minneapolis Mn, Corey grew up as an only child. Relentlessly bullied in grade school, he struggled to make friends and fit in. Looked at and defined by his teachers as a slow learner, he predominately struggled in math, but always excelled in reading and word comprehension. Graduating with an average G.P.A from Roosevelt High school in 1992, he only attended one year of college at Minnesota State University at Mankato before he eventually dropped out. Bouncing around from a variety of different jobs, he finally landed in the biopharmaceutical industry. For the next decade, Corey worked his way to upper management, where he ultimately was responsible for annual operating budgets of over 6 million dollars.

Corey did not realize until his mid-40's that he was an author. One day he sat down in front of his computer and started typing. Having never previously written anything else, Corey completed his first book La Familia Loose Ends in only three months. Corey attributes his love for writing to the feeling of freedom and escape it gives him. When he was asked about his inspiration for when he writes, Corey very simply states that the visions and images in his head come to life. And when they do, he feels compelled to write about them, or he will lose them forever.

www.ingramcontent.com/pod-product-compliance
Lightning Source LLC
Chambersburg PA
CBHW021040130626
46552CB00005B/1943